**ORIGINALS**

NEW WRITING FROM
BRITAIN'S OLDEST PUBLISHER

Risk-taking writing for risk-taking readers.

JM Originals was launched in 2015 to champion distinctive, experimental, genre-defying fiction and non-fiction. From memoirs and short stories to literary and speculative fiction, it is a place where readers can find something, well, *original*.

JM Originals is unlike any other list out there with its editors having sole say in the books that get published on the list. The buck stops with them and that is what makes things so exciting. They can publish from the heart, on a hunch, or because they just really, really like the words they've read.

Many Originals authors have gone on to win or be shortlisted for a whole host of prizes including the Booker Prize, the Desmond Elliott Award and the Women's Prize for Fiction. Others have been selected for promotions such as Indie Book of the Month. Our hope for our wonderful authors is that JM Originals will be the first step in their publishing journey and that they will continue writing books for John Murray well into the future.

Every JM Original is published with a limited-edition print run. This means every time you buy one of our covetable books, you're not only investing in an author's career but also building a library of (potentially!) valuable first editions. Writers need readers and we'd love for you to become part of our JM Originals community. Get in contact and tell us what you love about our books. We're waiting to hear from you.

Coming from JM Originals in 2021

Penny Baps | Kevin Doherty
A beautifully-told debut about the relationship between brothers and the difference between good and bad.

A Length of Road | Robert Hamberger
A memoir about love and loss, fatherhood and masculinity, and John Clare, by a Polari Prize -shortlisted poet.

We Could Not See the Stars | Elizabeth Wong
To discover the truth about his mother, Han must leave his village and venture to a group of islands which hold the answer to a long-held secret.

Penny Baps

Kevin Doherty

JM ORIGINALS

First published in Great Britain in 2021 by JM Originals
An Imprint of John Murray (Publishers)
An Hachette UK company

1

A CIP catalogue record for this title is available from the British Library

Trade Paperback ISBN 9781529348613
eBook ISBN 9781529348620

Typeset in Minion Pro 11.75/15 pt by Palimpsest Book Production Limited, Falkirk, Stirlingshire

Printed and bound in Great Britain by Clays Ltd, Elcograf S.p.A.

John Murray policy is to use papers that are natural, renewable and recyclable products and made from wood grown in sustainable forests. The logging and manufacturing processes are expected to conform to the environmental regulations of the country of origin.

John Murray (Publishers)
Carmelite House
50 Victoria Embankment
London EC4Y 0DZ

www.johnmurraypress.co.uk

The Trees

G oing over the lane at Carrick, Cahir's arms are on fire. The stone trail is slippy under fallen leaves, rotting brown and orange. His shoulders and forearms burn with the weight of carting two bin bags. Him trying to stop them dragging on the ground. The lane is narrow, like a tunnel, with the hedgerow reaching in and almost meeting over-head. The trees have dropped leaf, snaked with ivy and honeysuckle vine. In the dull of early winter the lane is still wrung with green, spliced with holly and lined in great busting sprays of fern.

He'd have slowed his step if it wasn't for the buzzing, the hum that has shown up to thrill through his nerves, pulling him tight. He shouldn't let a living thing dry out. The little stems he carries are the bones of something young, so easy to snap or starve, and Cahir counts the minutes that they're out of water, pores closed, their drive to suck suppressed. He hurries against the limits of survival.

Living in a battered place, he has learned to see those limits. To notice signs of struggle. Familiar with what's rough and hard, Cahir has learned to spot where something will grow. The soft and sheltered, protected and fertile strips that weave between ocean cliffs and high mountain bogs. Green corners and flat squares that can be turned to production, that can be fenced off and cultivated. In respite from the salty winds and Inner Seas, sheltered by sand dunes and beaten hills, there are pockets of growth that survive and Cahir hurries toward one of them.

On a stony track he knows well, he is alone, safe. The muscles around his jaw and cheeks soften out of a tiring arrangement. Away from eyes that follow and pick apart, Cahir is bodiless. He floats.

At the end of the lane, at the oxidised gate, he is level with the steeple and the clocktower and the chimneys of the town, stacked, clambering on Barrack Hill, two miles east. With his back to the town, the ground slips down and away from Cahir. A gradual slope to a rocky stream and then a hill lifting quickly, a long ridge, a hump that shelters the town from the brutal west. He knows that the back and shoulders of the hill are covered in heather, turning purple, turning brown, but from the gate he can't see it. From here it's only the woods he can see, a sweeping canopy of leaf-bare oak. It climbs over the whole face of the hill. High, thriving and forgotten. A swathe, a slip of what's untouched, untroubled, rare and good.

Cahir is coming to work at a scrap of rushes belonging

to his mother. Five wet acres she was left by poor Sean the Yelper, her virgin uncle. The Yelpers have abandoned the land. Generations and generations dependent on it until finally they could stop working so hard. None of them are farmers now. Teachers and engineers. Civil servants and accountants. They've progressed far from the dirt and cruelty of having to survive on the land like that. Marie wasn't first in line to get Uncle Sean's bit of earth and the word was that Sean had a soft spot for Graham, a husband blown in from Dunree. Cahir's mum was happy to have beaten out her cousins but she hardly gave the land another thought. The Yelper inheritance was easily forgotten, thought useless apart from the associated turbary rights and they did cut turf for a few seasons, for the novelty, for the laugh about turning and footing and throwing the sods. Laughing at the bags of turf they dragged home, dried out sticks of hollowed muck. Cahir didn't think the turf was that funny. He didn't forget that the hill was owned in common, shared by the landowners under it. That the Yelper scrap of rushes gave them a share of the western hill and the bog-encircled woods.

Cahir isn't sure his plan will work and until he's sure he will keep his head down. Keep quiet. In preparation, the best he could do was sit and watch. He sat through years of comings and goings, of the rhythms that mark out the use of a place. The Masters and the Oregons own the neighbouring fields, they share the common hill, but only the Masters keep animals and they don't stray as far as this. Not when they have so much good grass close to the byres.

Inside the gate and parallel to the lane, there is a strip

of thinner darker growth where the fields were torn up for new power lines. A rerouting across the hill so that the supply in Woodtop would be secure. The Yelpers agreed to an easement. They allowed the ESB to come in with a few wooden poles and with twisting heavy wires that track the lane. A brief intrusion and forgotten again. Let back to seed, more grass and rushes. They ripped up some whin bushes when they stuck in their masts and they left them overturned, drying out in heaps, like cinder wood after a fire, a sentry line of dead mounds to separate what's ruined and what's whole. That violence is Cahir's chance. The cleared and churned earth can be put to better use, restored.

Inside the gate, he has hidden his tools. A barrow and spade and a bag of well-rotted manure. A ball of twine and some bamboo canes. A watering can pre-filled to brimming from the iron pump at the main road. Cahir rests the saplings against a stand of rushes. He paces the earth, muck squelching beneath him, and makes for the spade.

They were selling the wee trees at the top of the Church Road, at the High Cross next to the Protestant graveyard. The Cross is a remnant of a holy site and it was an appropriate spot for the assembled crowd, shaping for virtue, competing with the figures chipped into stone, determined and pious, like the Three Holy Women going to the tomb. A notch in the main road, with space to park two cars, it was the site of a monastery and an early church, all trampled and cleared and buried deep under layers and layers of compacted fill. Cambered tar sweeping up from the river, from the town and the school, past the edge of Cahir's lane and the woods.

Cahir saw salvation proclaimed in the supermarket. A Native Tree Sale by the Inishowen Environmental Society. A limp poster in faded colour and decorated with the bough of a Clipart tree, it's how he knew to be waiting. Long before the advertised start time, Cahir and a crowd of cunning operators loitered at the Cross, keen to get roots in the ground before the ground froze.

Don't buy crabapple if you know what's good for you, they warned each other from under hoods.

I'd count sycamore a weed, one said.

Not right native either, said another.

Cahir suffered their outpourings quietly. He kept busy at the low granite wall where the saplings were laid in black bin bags, in groups according to their common names.

While hovering at a bag of sessile oak, counting stems, a lady sneaked up on him, dying to know was he OK there? Did he know what he was looking for?

Cahir jumped at the noise so close to his ear. He startled at the nearness of her face and her mass of greying hair. A bush, a halo of frizz, each strand of hair coarse and static and unable to lie flat. Cahir quickly arranged a huge smile. I'm fine for now, he said, all sunny. Thank you though.

She wouldn't catch Cahir as handy as that. They can never just stick to silence. What about a bit of manners? What about don't be prying? Fucking hell. It's true, aye, that Cahir has no proven success in horticulture. True, and obvious to look at him maybe, that his record of nurture is short and fatal but if that was her final assessment then good luck to her, the dolt.

Cahir is going to take care of the trees and that's why it's not the same as the parsley in the orange pot, which was ages ago, and which was only for garnishes, and which Cahir would never claim could save the world, or any corner of it. The Doherty family just weren't in the habit of garnishing their plates. They were too eager to get them cleaned. Too hungry. Knives and forks and spoons never resting until every shovelful was swallowed. So the parsley sat on the kitchen windowsill and died. Withered. Starved. Crisped. It was sitting a long time dead before Marie thought to remove it, and Cahir never discovered the exact cause of death, he only knew that there had been some terrible and costly lack of attention. It must be Graham and Marie's fault that he was thick about these things. If they could have been the kind of parents who put fresh herbs into the dinner, or kept a dog, or cat, or even a goldfish for the boys to practise on, who knows what things the two brothers might have reared. But Graham and Marie never chanced a pet because they were very busy. Too busy for things like pets and gardens. Just look at the hedge up at home, on Molly's Brae, over-clipped and windburnt. Look at the two haggard shrubs stunted in the gravel, gasping. Cahir and Dan were lucky to come out near thriving.

Cahir went up and down the line quickly, looking to get away in good time. He was turning red, he could feel it. Burning at the thought they might know him, generally aware of him as one of Marie the Yelper's boys. You know. Her that married your man out of Dunree. They might year by year have watched him take his big fat grown-up shape. It wasn't fair that they would know him. An asymmetric advantage when he knows nobody. He had to get going. He had to get away quick.

At the bench below the Cross, where pilgrims sit in adoration, Cahir looked at the paper notes in his hand and tried to count what money could buy. He thought sixty euro was a very good price for being sinless. Only one sin mattering to Cahir when the whole earth was on fire. When we have the fires lit and spreading and burning everywhere. Cahir had to say sorry for being bad. For being alive in a world overrun. For the smouldering coals that trail about on his boots, a trampling wrecker. For his every breath in time with all the others, like bellows at an ember. He was going to dig at the ground with all his might, labour at the only small patch he can claim to own. To know if he can make it better. If his hands can do anything but wreck. It was sixty euro out the gate, sixty all in, and if he could keep it to sixty he'd be doing rightly. Sixty would be decent value for a chance to die in grace.

That hope roused Cahir, raised a smile and set him humming, even with the pains in his belly firing as he came to the curving yellow pebbledash of the graveyard wall. A tiny graveyard for Protestants, where left-footers and flat stone slabs weather bare, sinking in and around the monks' Marigold Stone, and where the footpath curves around the wall, and where its kerb crumbles into dust at the road. Smiling, as he came opposite the long white face of the Masters' farmhouse, too warm in his blue overcoat and muttering to himself about transpiration. About filtered soot and stuck carbon and general absolution, like you get at the Christmas penitential service. If the trees take, if they survive and grow, his life can be forgiven. If he plants enough of them, he can save Dan too, reclaim innocence for the two of them.

With that thought he battered on, sharpish, hoping to confuse nosey beaks with an air of purpose. There was nothing for it but purpose now the trees' delicate crowns were brushing the sides of his thighs, now the clouds swole a threat above the Mountain Road.

Cahir steps out the planting area, trying to imagine the trees grown high, as tall as those across the stream, a new canopy rising over the stream border of holly and rowan trees. The idea is that they should form a sort of copse of their own. A natural-looking group like a spur from the old woods. A daring spasm of youth that just couldn't sit still, that just couldn't be tied and that leapt over rocks and streams, no bother on them.

That fancy lasts a right while. It's what got Cahir this far. It lasts right up until the first swing of his spade. Right up until that dull thud.

He should have dug the holes yesterday.

It's the first of the day's lessons and the others aren't slow behind. Cahir soon learns that digging holes is not that easy; holy fuck it's not easy. It's an activity for a man wriggling with those wee muscles that harden at your command. A man with coarse skin on his hands. It is going to be a day's work in itself because everywhere he sticks the spade's cutting edge is rock. His is a stony, watery sanctuary that would have benefited from a thorough mapping exercise. Or a riven plough. It's a matter of inching, of standing on the tread of the spade, of finding the spot where the blade will sink.

When he has the rim of a hole cut and the soil tipped, he tries to get his fingers to the flat grey stones, shaking and pulling as if they have roots of their own. He beats down on the stones with the blade and cuts at them from outside the hole, trying to find the far side of them.

With a passable depth excavated he stumbles to his bin bag and pulls out a hawthorn. It can go in first because it only needs a small hole. It is a tiny thing altogether. A spiky wee stalk only as high as his knee. There are no hawthorns in the proper woods but Cahir wants them as a marker. So people know they're on the edge of something. That they're leaving behind what's used up. That there is a limit to the wrecked world.

Cahir has been coming to the woods since Graham told his best story one Sunday on the way back from Buncrana.

His dad said every week that he couldn't understand, how in this day and age, there wasn't a swimming pool in a town the size of Carn. As if the day and age were deserving. Marie came the odd Sunday but mostly it was Graham and Cahir and Dan. All the boys rinsing in the showers, swimming caps and goggles and flip-flops to separate them from the white square tiles and the wet, dark, grout. Sometimes there were floats or lilos but even with no inflatables the boys were happy near the shallow end, splashing in the echoing hall and treading water. Cahir had learned how to do the breaststroke in PE class and felt it was important to show Dan what he knew. After the lessons, Dan always wanted to race. It wasn't fair to race when Cahir was five years older and when Dan was small even for eight years old, but Dan made up for the gap in size with lightness and a serious engine. He would shoot over the top of the water, hardly sunk at all, churning water in a mad front crawl, and if he was trailing behind, he would pull at Cahir's foot or try and break Cahir's stroke.

It was a twenty-five metre pool. Graham swam twenty laps every week, and they wouldn't have stopped him short of a drowning. Since he'd given up the football, Graham had got very into swimming and running. He was training for some kind of long race. Cahir kept a general eye on how many bodies were in the pool. He watched Graham's laps, counting his every return to the shallow end, his fingertips outstretched and his roll forward to kick out from the wall. Cahir took to the changing room early to get his hair washed and his body dried and hidden while the changing rooms were quiet.

He had to get his bag organised and get into the toilet cubicle before anybody saw. Flip-flops were very important then because there could be piss on the tiles. He folded his clothes on top of the cistern and on the closed seat of the bowl. Space was very limited and it was hard to get completely dry before dressing. Often, he would be pulling socks on to damp feet, wriggling from the horrible warmth of the T-shirt sticking to wet patches on his back.

He couldn't stay out in the open changing room where the men weren't covered or smoothed over. Their bare features sticking out under wet hair. The strange contours of their humped backs and sunken chests emerging from clouds of deodorant. Nothing covered up. Not even dicks.

In his mid-forties then, Graham had a full head of greying blond hair and was physically exact in a way which made him look younger. A tall, strong figure of a man, trim and kept from all the running and swimming, he sometimes put on his socks before his pants. Cahir wondered at them all walking about in no hurry to cover up. Relaxed towelling down their backs and in between grisly toes. He didn't understand how they could show themselves like that. He didn't believe he could be one of them and the thought that he should be, or that he had to be, was so strange that it must be wrong. It was impossible.

Cahir was allowed to spend a fiver in the tuck shop after the swim and that's where he headed. Better to get out of the heat of the changing room. Better to forget about bodies and get into the fresh air. A fiver went a long way in that shop. Stinger bars and Refreshers and candy smokes were dirt cheap and there wasn't a dick in sight. They were so cheap that he would buy one bar for the drive home and one to eat immediately on the wall under the convent school. It was on one of those drives down the Mountain Road, over Lough Namin and the rocky hills crowned King and Queen of the Mintiaghs, that his dad said, Maybe we'll cut turf this year, lads. What do yous reckon?

Cahir was pretending to read *The Murder of Roger Ackroyd* and to ignore the fear that reared in him, that he would be too fat to foot turf, too girly and soft, nibbling his bubblegum Refresher bar.

Where would *we* cut turf? Cahir asked eventually. Sure they were townies from Molly's Brae, not Craignahorna or Meenahoner.

We used to cut turf over there, said Graham, waving his hand generally across the rolling heather as they came to the mountain lakes. The Yelpers have a stake in that area because of the land at Carrick. Your mum's land, he said.

Mum doesn't have any land, Cahir said, eyes now well raised from the page.

And what, your mum was stealing turf, was she? Her and your granny Callaghan?

Cahir was stuck. Snookered. Granny the Yelper was a woman of stout morals and would never be thieving turf.

Dan never lifted his eyes from his console, his thumbs tapping vigorously, frowning, sighing, hissing. Cahir knew Dan was having trouble getting past the robo-pirates. He knew about the different levels and bosses and the general progress of the quest, but he couldn't settle back into Rayman or Roger Ackroyd now that he was a landowner. Now that he had a share in the wild areas above the town.

Cahir refills the soil around the roots and stands on the loose earth, firming it in around the finger-thick trunks. He likes the sight of them. The three hawthorns set in beside each other, a close triangle that will blossom together, a great mass of white. He stands back and pumps his fist, tripping across the slope in excitement, banging into the metal watering-can, stirring a couple of birds in the high canopy. He watches as they flutter and circle and come back down. That'll be lovely, he says to himself, quieter. Plausible too, he thinks. Not an obvious fake.

Cahir is tired. Two or three holes might have done for a first day digging. But naw. Cahir tears the bags open and drags them along as he moves across the soil, hunched, wild, staggering them as best the earth will let him. Clawing the holes open with his hands in an imperfect design. Physical labour takes all thought from him and he'll be easy rocked tonight if he can just own more than a litter of dead things.

Even without his overcoat and his woollen jumper the sweat is lashing him, blinding him, and his heavy twill shirt is sticking to him. The stones he can get out, he uses to weigh down the manure as he heaps it in over refilled soil, stamping into the earth around each stem. A wandering, bare-looking grove of tiny spikes follows him, skinny sticks in pools of black manure, dwarfed by the starved and drying ruins of dead boughs and roots.

Cahir's hands are filthy, manure and soil are gathered under his nails and the broken and dislodged rubble dyes the creases in his palms. He looks at them until he has a breath back but then he keeps going. That's what he will say for himself. His knees are soaked and his cords are clattered because he didn't bring anything to wipe the muck on but he keeps going and he does get them all in the ground; ash and oak, holly, birch and hawthorn, and he waters them in even though rain is forecast and not far away, because they need a good drink.

*

It is hard to believe it only took three hours. Cahir is in a daze. His face is numb bar a circle of localised tingling. An aura of dots swarms in his eyes. It's an interesting array of neurological warning signs as the buzzing builds. He hides his bits and pieces at the edge of the lane and walks home with his hands in his pockets to hide the dirt of them. He is smeared in damp soil from the waist down but he can't hide that. His boots are caked around the edges and dripping muck from under the soles in a trail of incomplete prints. He wipes them on the verge as best he can before appearing on the public footpath. Numb all over in a way that doesn't feel like triumph, worrying that he did it wrong. He's worrying about the tingling in his cheek and the waving aura that won't recede and what Graham once said about high winds and tying down things that you care about. He'll have to be over weeding and watering them every other day. Forking in compost and bone-meal. Adding to them every year because reproduction is a part of persistence and they are too small to have a strategy. Until they can throw copies on the wind or drop a tempting berry, Cahir is all they have. He's a required nuisance until they can be sure of lasting, high on the confidence of a three-metre trunk.

Twenty-five minutes' walk and he's home, burned through, emptied of the force he needs to kick off his boots. He steps out of his cold, stiff cords, peels off his muddy socks, and throws them in the drum of the washing machine.

He won't tell Dan about the trees yet. In the spring maybe, when he knows if they're living or dead. Cahir is the right man for a secret. The great secrets of the world are best kept by fat boys and girls. Fat boys like Cahir with no shortage of capacity or cover or practice, the ones who've been hoarding for years, building heft in the quiet when backs were turned.

Cahir can hear Dan in the sitting room, shouting at FIFA. He closes the bathroom door and gets in the shower. Happy to get clean.

The only niggle is the pain in his belly. The strain of walls stretched thin by fullness, of skin pulled taut at the limits of elasticity. Visceral girth is a complicating factor and Cahir has read all about weak spots and herniation. He read that sometimes your gut pops out through your belly button. Cahir is very quick to notice new pain. In general, his life is ordered to avoid it. To be safe even from the fear of it. As the hot water falls and the muck drains away he tries to remember old pains and how long it took them to go away. It's probably normal after so much digging, he thinks.

He is clean and tired. He stretches side to side, tilting his spine one way and then the other. Resetting after all his work. Content with the new proof of himself and the ground he broke open with a twist of his back.

In the sitting room, Cahir will have to ask a few times before Dan turns off the PlayStation. Then they'll sit about for the afternoon, the evening and into the night, watch a film maybe. Sometimes they watch two. Dan will read through the options and ask Cahir to pick. In the end, Cahir will make Dan choose. Cahir will cook the dinner and Dan will light the fire. He'll bring over the logs and the coal from the shed, making several trips to fill the white plastic buckets. He'll empty the ashes and fiddle the draughts and warm the sitting room even after Cahir says no. Don't. Pretending that he's too warm as it is. Roasting. That he's suffocated with the heat. In a sky too full of smoke already.

The Milkshed

It is the broad *a* that rings from the landing, the held ending of her name that echoes through the upstairs hall. Lydia doesn't bother calling back because she can hear Dolly's footsteps on the stairs, coming to her. She is at the doorway, her face all serious feeling, waiting for Lydia to enquire from the edge of her bed. It's not a contest her mother can win when the news weighs so heavy on her.

You'll never guess who's after dying, she says.

It's one of Dolly's games. Not Lydia's favourite but certainly a classic: Guess Who's Dead. There must be nobody in the house because Dolly normally prefers to play with Sam or Tom, or over the phone with Charlie in Effish. Lydia has too poor a grasp on local dynasties to be a competent player. They all have too many connections, too many relations, it would take all the space in her head to keep them accurate and updated. She wishes they could settle the rules of the game in advance, like, is there a time limit?

Maybe if you gave me a proper clue for once, she says.

Dolly frowns like this isn't what she wanted at all. Lydia is making fun and at a time like this. It's not on. Not when Vincent Tim is dead. Through no fault in Dolly, or the solemnity of her in proclamation, the news doesn't land with any special gravity. Lydia shakes her head,

Who's he?

Big Vincie Tim. What a man. Didn't he sell cattle at the mart with daddy for twenty-odd years? Sure wasn't he a *tonic*?

Definitely no and probably not. Dolly is a great collector of stories but not an accurate transmitter of them.

Dead, she says. Dolly finds it hard to fathom how someone can just drop. A massive heart attack, Dr Foley is saying. And poor Kate will miss him wile. Lydia makes the start of a wince and a wince is what's too much for Dolly.

You've met Kate manys a time. You know her, Lydia. I know you know her. She'd be a great big fat woman?

Her with the wile-looking blue rinse?

It's easier to pretend and Poor Kate, as she shall now be known, was at Slimming World in Moville, trying to count her sins. She told Vincie to get back into bed if he was that sick. You'd say she shouldn't have gone but Vincie was up and dressed so how was Kate to know? He told her Patsy McCandless was outside waiting with her lift and would she not get a move on? Poor Kate only lost half a pound, Dolly says, and Lydia thinks Patsy McCandless is some bitch to betray Slimming World secrets like that.

Kate was home, says Dolly, coming in the back door when she saw Vincie's feet poking from under the counter. She tried her might to rouse him but there was no rousing Vincie.

Lydia laughs. Oh my God, Mum, she says, don't tell it like that.

Like what?

Like it's funny.

It's not a bit funny, he was only sixty-eight in May and the men used to céilí two or three nights a week with him. It's a wake on us anyway.

No way, Lydia says. I don't know them. Where's Tom? He'll go if it's a farming crowd.

Dolly is deadly serious about a wake. Death and cake are the things to take most seriously. She's away down now to make tea scones. If in doubt, make a few treacle tea scones because they'll hardly go to waste. Dolly's treacle scones are generally acclaimed and she has learned that when asked for two dozen buns it's better to send two dozen and four.

On the edge of her bed, at the open window, the air has turned fresh. Lydia is wrapped against the cold with her feet in warm slippers. She leaves the window open as often as she can because the glass condenses at the northern end of the house, obscuring her view. Lydia is watching the clouds from a certain height. It's just the right height to see underneath them and to bet on whether they'll hold their water or burst. The view of the sky from her old bedroom is one of the things Lydia knows best in the world.

The front face of their house is a public space, the

trellises smothered in roses and other climbers, bordering the main road to the sea. They share the site with the yellow Protestant church, the High Cross and the Marigold Stone. They share their land with strange words and figures carved in stone. It's hard to believe with three roads meeting but this is a pilgrimage site. They say the house was in a bad state when Dolly came from Effish, glory mingling with wedding bells as she arrived under the arch of the front door. That the poor house hadn't a look in with Sam's mother dying so young and his father so busy at the cattle.

Dolly wasn't afraid of a bit of work. In Effish her own mother had taught her and her sisters how to graft. In the yard with the animals, at the fire with the turf, on their knees scrubbing tiles and scrubbing them again. And here at least, Dolly could scrub her own floors in a house worth saving. A six-bay, two-storey farmhouse at the edge of the town. Dolly yanked it up, straightened it out, she put all to right in the house and none of that was any effort to Dolly because she's a born worker, pulling them in around her and her store of treacle scones.

Lydia was happy before she got the death notice. The cold tightening her into something more like perfect and much less alive. Downstairs, she'll be forced to warm up, rearrange herself in the heat, assume her old role as the girl who grew up in these rooms, a reliable fixture, a shimmering and consistent image they all know by heart. Warming herself at the open fire, it will be like she never left.

Tom comes in through the kitchen extension. Lydia hears

him shake off his boots at the scullery step and open the latch door into the middle kitchen. The lid of the pot rattles on the cooker and he rises a bowl from the dresser. Lunch of leftover soup and a few spuds boiled last night. Big Tommy the Master. He's the man for you. Accountant, corner-back and part-time farmer. Her brother the dote, he never sits. Their dad still tinkers about the farmyard but he leaves most of it to Tom now. Sam says there's too much science in it these days. That it's gone over his head. It's more that he'd rather his head applied elsewhere. Sam is working on a history of the Carndonagh Mart and the Inishowen Co-Operative Society and has a seat on at least three industrious committees. He tried to preserve the routines he inherited but there's only so much you can get done in an evening. He milked the cows before work and after work but eventually he switched away from dairy. He closed the petrol pump in the yard and silenced the bell calling to the house because Dolly hated the smell of petrol on her hands. Their right name is Doherty but they get 'the Master' after some relation of Sam's who ran a hedge school in Malin Head. The name suited Sam because he ended up headmaster of the gurriers in Carn and they all take the name now, even when none of them are teachers. Lydia the Master, Tomas the Master, and Dolly too, all on their own piece of the earth, a sweep of mixed ground as far as Moore's Glen and it is natural for them to stay together when they have so much space.

Tom is working at a boundary fence, Lydia thinks. She saw the coils of shiny silver wire laid out on the grass, waiting to be strung tight between clean posts. On a cool day, with a job of work done, it would be nice to get home for soup and spuds. It would be nice to fit so well in a certain place. Tom is solid and right-looking at the scullery step in his wellies, at the slatted sheds in the yard, at the kitchen table, grinding pepper into his tin bowl.

Dressed and downstairs, Lydia walks past Tom and on to Dolly in the top sitting room, dusting with a bottle of polish. The scones are in the oven already.

Did you tell Tom about your man Vincie?

How could I tell him? He never has that phone on him. I don't know why he bothers with a phone at all.

Lydia goes back through and sits opposite Tom, tracing her finger over the knots and patterns of the wood.

Did you hear about Vincent Tim?

Naw, what?

Dead. Massive heart attack.

Fuck, he says.

So Dr Foley said. Kate was out at Slimming World and he just dropped. Mum says you have to go to the wake. They're going as soon as Dad gets in.

I have football, Tom says, but I can go after. Or, what time is the removal?

Lydia calls up to the other room. Mum? What time is the removal?

I don't know. I was waiting on Dad home.

Lydia finds the confirmation online. You're not really dead until you're listed among the Highland Radio obituaries. She stands under the architrave, between the two rooms, and reads aloud to both Dolly and Tom.

The death has taken place at his late residence of Vincent McLaughlin (Tim), Corvish, Carndonagh, husband of Kate and brother of Gary, Joanne and Noel. Remains reposing at his late residence from 6 p.m. Monday the 10th of November. The funeral Mass will take place on Wednesday at 11 a.m. in the Church of the Sacred Heart, Carndonagh, with burial afterwards in the adjoining cemetery. Family only from 11 p.m. to 11 a.m. and on the morning of the funeral. Family flowers only please, donations in lieu of flowers if desired to the Irish Heart Foundation.

You'll have to go after football, Lydia says.

Tom sort of grunts, re-filling his bowl and putting two more potatoes on his side plate. He peels them at the table and the skin comes off easy. They are big dry floury spuds, made for thickening a bowl of soup.

Would you ever do anything with that house? That's all Lydia hears from Dolly.

Dolly would love if Lydia had a plan. If she could decide about her life. What she wants and how to get it. She's old enough now at twenty-four. Dolly would just like to know if Lydia is going to stay. If she's back for ever.

The cottage needs a fortune spent on it but it could be lovely. A two-bedroom cottage that belonged to her Auntie Bee, Sam's sister. The only thing 'of any significance' she had to leave in her will. That's what the solicitor said.

It's horrible to be singled out with a gift that can't be repaid. Lydia's in the red with Auntie Bee and there is no way to make it up. A debt to the dead was enough to make Lydia research the technicalities of refusal. Disclaiming a bequest. But gradually she understood that Bee had no one else to leave it to. It was the only rational response to the tax code and the favourite niece or nephew exemption. Father Michael would have got it more than likely.

Just keep her in your prayers. That was Dolly's advice.

Mum, I'm being serious, said Lydia. What will I do?

So am I, Dolly said. That's what she'd want from you. She hasn't many others to think of her.

And then Dolly cried for all the good she did. Stern Sister Bee, the matron of the ward, home alone after thirty years in Connecticut to be buried at the bottom of Millbrae. They heard of a man in America at one stage but it's unlikely he thinks of Bee now, and anyway, divorced Protestants mightn't know any of the best prayers.

However Lydia considers it, however hard she could make herself pray, it's an unfair swap for a faltering show of consideration. A back and forth in long-delayed letters and a three-day visit when Lydia went to New York on a summer work visa. There should be a bigger price for lattice windows and carved bargeboards. It'll take a fortune to save but the ridge cresting might deserve it. It might be worth staying about for and that's what she's afraid of. Whatever life Lydia had, wherever she lived it, she might never have four prettier rooms or as big a patch of garden. Big enough for a small glasshouse where she could be picking, potting and hardening on all year. A big stretch of a garden and the

24

field behind it. What they call the Well Field for a spring that bubbles on low ground. The Well Field that climbs in a narrow strip to join the farm at Carrick. Less than a mile from home, on the same sweep of the road and under the same hill, that could be her, Lydia the lottery winner choosing between samples of lime plaster, trying not to be wooed by the cheaper cementitious render.

It's hard to believe now that she's home. Fine Art in Belfast. Pissing about with aluminium plates and ink prints, with blown-up rough patches, framed distortions. It's an embarrassing story now that it's over. Lydia was able to content herself with charcoal pencils in embossed milk jars because if she hadn't been left the cottage, then her and Tom will eventually split the home house. Or she'll be left one of the fields close to the Cross, or a share of the money made safe over years and seasons. They were offered 800,000 euro for a field near the new bypass and you don't forget figures like that no matter how you try. Lydia can't apologise for these things because they're out of her choosing, like the high bones in her cheeks.

You're my Number One. That's what Bee used to whisper in her ear, loud enough for the room to hear. Stand there on that diamond, she used to say, pointing to the pink and brown carpet, and then she would grab Lydia and kiss her on her cheek with wet, blowing, unpractised kisses. Lydia would never have taken the backhanded cash if she knew there was a lump sum coming. She tries to forget about the wee house and the lovely bargeboards, but on the ledger of things worth living for, they're a weight.

Lydia went to Belfast and found that she wasn't an artist.

That she had nothing to say. No response to a place of grizzled movement and trapped nerves. She honestly didn't care about the pains of war. She retreated into tiny cracks. Pictures of flaking paint and rough plaster. Inconsequential faults blown up so they were like moonscapes. The little wrinkles were what she noticed and she set them in materials that would last.

After the course finished, without direction or deadlines, she stopped making things and nobody cared. Nobody needed the things Lydia made. She lost access to the workshops and machinery. She hated Fran anyway. And Oliver and Holly. She was glad that they were moving out of the house, glad they were leaving Belfast. She was spiteful and glad to feel their absence. She poked and teased the empty space for the ache it gave her. She had nothing but that ache. She looked at herself and saw nothing. Cared for nothing. The things she had believed in were only ghosts around her. Stupid, false things, not solid enough to pick up and examine. Not real enough to need burying.

Lydia got very bored of her aching body and its sleepless routine. The same attempt to do something different and then the same bellyful of whatever would bring a quick riptide to her legs. The rush past the point of sense, the falling whoosh and drag, pulling out to sea and to some minor oblivion. The feel of a man she didn't know between her legs, fighting to stay awake, to say yes in consent, so he would fuck her. So she could be of use to somebody. Do something.

Half memories of a stairwell she couldn't climb. Of a fire on the hob and the burns she gave herself. Bruises and cuts too. Of the kind man in a glowing coat and the double yellow lines in Shaftesbury Square. He scraped her up, barely responsive, overly sedate on the ground outside a chipper named Spudz. She had been trying to go to the cinema, to see if she would sleep if she had a very soft chair. Hanging on to a metal collar around a lime tree, slipping down and lying there in her summer dress, cut from her body, almost from everything.

It wasn't a sign of distress, it was just a mistake. Lydia pulled the cannula out of her own vein and smiled her way off the ward, a trickle of blood running down the inside of her arm. She told Dolly she was coming home. She was going to sort out Bee's house. Deal with the inheritance. That was the official story. The excuse. She was just sorry they had paid for the degree already. It was a lot of money to play dress-up. For them to say she was special when she's not.

At the back of the house, across the yard, the converted milkshed is where Lydia spent her weekends through secondary school. Scratching with pencils, editing photos, doodling on the big sloping lid, scored all over with pen marks, the names of students scraped into the wood and filled with ink. Lydia loved that the lid lifted up and that the space beneath was large enough for copybooks and fragments of paper, for torn edges of colour or any scrap of nonsense. The shed is a great storage space. All her unsold works leaning on each other, metal plates, original photos, final prints, they slot between the desk and the cold unpainted walls, they are screened by the blue metal door, corrugated and hung, sliding on its galvanised track.

In the little garden behind the hayshed, some ragwort is just dying back. She'll pull it out when she's helping Dolly lift the dahlias. Up close, there are always dead heads to pinch. They will flower for another while and then she'll lift them because they're not hardy and you can't fault them for unforgiving ground. Over the weeds, Dolly's orchard. Only a slice of an orchard. Just Reverend Wilks, Herefordshire Beefing and Arthur Turner. Lydia would love to add a Perry Pear and the thought of another timetable eases her. She'd enjoy watching over them for a late frost that kills the blossoms, or the first ripe fruit on the top of a stepladder. A windfall she could have with no effort. The days have got short and the best rays of the sun are long before bed. Lydia wants to sweep up the light and make a wrap of it but Dolly is shouting from the back door.

Lydia! Come in out of there now. You'll catch your death. For God's sake, Dolly says. Charles and Mary B are landed. Will you come in and watch the stew?

The John McGinley bus trundles past the Cross and swings out toward Ballyliffin on the long way to Derry and then Dublin. You can get anywhere on the McGinley bus. The orange top of it barrels away from Lydia and she passes no remark.

Walking back over the yard, she skims her boots on the holes in the concrete, forming like algae on a lake, battered out by the rain. The rain falling every which way and eroding until someone re-paves. Whoever that will be. Inside at the scullery sink, Lydia doesn't want to talk just yet. She gets scissors from the cutlery drawer and cuts a sprig of thyme from the jug on the windowsill, for the stew, in case White Haired Mary stays for dinner.

A Forecast

L ife roots in the gaps that form as rock edges fray, chip
and slough. Cahir's rocks seem to start at the ditch and
proliferate from there. From the banks of the stream they
spread into the field, are strewn throughout the soil, the
soil only thinly masking the stones. The rushes have turned
brown and red and they don't mind damp feet. They don't
mind the rocks. Early in the morning, Cahir is over and
back before Dan is out of bed.

The easiest way into the proper woods is at the Mass
Rock. A stone cross painted white but turning green at the
edges. A cross on a rock above a small metal bowl for donations. Wishes. The bowl has filled with water and a few red
holly berries are floating. Without a verger on the books,
there is nobody to collect donations. The coins are left in
the bowl, wet and rusting.

From the clearing under the altar you keep walking into

the trees, fending off the understorey ringed in scrambling holly. The woods are made of oak and under them the floor is soft and damp, covered in mottled litter and huge rolling pillows of bright green moss. Thick carpets of moss make cosy cloaks and high socks on all the trunks and stumps. Growing on the wet sides of every old tree there is Tamarisk moss and big shaggy moss. Ferns growing on the upside of the branches. The moisture held in the mosses enough to feed them. Cahir has learned to pick names from the general green. It took time for his eyes to get used to small differences. It took a bit of looking before he knew what was what. Until he could see woodrush in the sward or the splatter of lungwort sprouting on the barks. It is an oceanic oak wood. Rare and at risk.

As Cahir wanders down his gentle slope, away from the lane and the gate, he is calmed to see the slow and quiet growth of the woods. To hear the intermittent drip from the canopy, the birds tweeting even in November. He responds in his breath and his pulse and the movement of his eyes. He becomes a little more like them, a little more solid as he tries to breathe them in. He will never leave this place. He doesn't have a choice when his organs are defective. Some sort of malformation deep in the lungs that has left him unable to breathe any other air. No other air feeds him but this air. Without it, there's no replenishment, only gradual expiration and desaturation. Lungs so diseased that the air off Dunaff is all he can tolerate. He is made of this place and without it he would be unmade. Sawn, cropped. A harvesting of roots and suckers. A transplant too much like butchery.

Every day Cahir comes back, he expects the trees to be gone or to be broken or to be torn out and finished. As he walks to Carrick, he practises their dying and how he'll explain it. How he'll handle the blame. He comes to the gate always in fear but every day they are still there. All where he put them, safe above the stream and below the power lines. The sounds are of cattle lowing, answering each other, and of the cars on the road, but Cahir is in the wild, alone and unwatched, and the noises mean nothing.

Back in the kitchen, a woman from Met Éireann says it's raining. Her drawl is automated but it is pleasant to hear her give warnings to the small crafts about the coasts or out on the Irish Sea. The pressure is falling slowly in Malin Head, she says, but from their height on Molly's Brae the two boys can see the clouds for miles and there is no sign of rain. Cahir hopes the predicted fronts are only late to prevail and that he'll see them yet. He would hate to have a scientific model undermined. Above them, the road climbs into the higher bogs but below them the town is obvious, splat, on a plain that runs in bumps to two different seas. On a clear day over the town and the plain they can see the Paps of Jura, and Cahir is fond of the glamour in that. Rounded hills circle the low plain with spits and humps of bog. Rocky juts and irregular spines run through it, fenced off in small dormant squares where the grass has very slowly turned. Looking at a thing every day Cahir didn't notice the slide into dormancy after the silage was saved. Cut and baled or dumped in the pit and covered, weighed down with old tyres, doused and pickling. The wind is blowing in over the town. It's blowing wild and for Cahir that's a sustenance story. That it's a great luxury to breathe that air skitting in at him, merciless, in a fine empty space.

Dan comes into the kitchen, wearing just a pair of shorts and Cahir sits up straight, hiking his shoulders and withdrawing the folds of his belly because Dan's chest is tight and lean and he has some hair on it already. Cahir sniffs his fingertips and sticks his nose into his armpits but the damp earth is soaped away and the only smell is spotlessness. Dan is rattling drawers, banging cupboards, slathering chocolate spread on to burnt toast, not a bit worried about simple sugars. A body can either tolerate Nutella or it can't. A man's body is heavy with tits and belly rings, or a man is lean and tall and upright, one happy shuffle of traits.

It's a fairly nice house. Average for the town. The only house the boys know. It's one and a half storeys on Molly's Brae next to Cannys' and McDermotts'. A strip of houses at the foot of the Mountain Road.

Upstairs the ceilings lean, squeezed under the eaves, but downstairs the rooms are square and regular. Everything is painted white. The walls, ceilings, the old pine furniture too. Down the hall from the kitchen, the big bedroom is Dan's but it was Cahir's first. For a time it was shared by the two boys until Cahir moved next door. Dan threw a huff when Cahir was moving but Cahir had to go once Barry Kline told him it was gay to share a room with his brother.

Looking at Dan, Cahir is proud because, deep down, they

are made of the same stuff, and because he thinks the final result is partly his doing. It was all the schooling. Upstairs, next to his mum and dad's bedroom, there is a box room they call an office. When the boys were small, they say Cahir ran a school in that room. That he would call the roll and Dan would answer from the floor, stick his hand in the air and shout *Anseo*! They say that Cahir led Dan around. That he carted Dan everywhere he went and they wondered how Cahir could carry him for so long when Dan was such a heavy toddler. A bruiser who loved his food. They called Cahir Elephant Ears because he heard everything and forgot nothing. They called him Bossy Boots because he was a very strict teacher, in bad temper if his pupil broke the rules. Once, Dan drew all over the sitting-room wall and said another boy did it. A bad boy they couldn't see called Humphrey. Cahir wanted to punish a lie but he couldn't hold out against Dan's tears.

Cahir will stay in the house until the end of next summer but then he'll have to go. When Dan's year out is over, Cahir will be gone.

Nobody expected the last-minute deferral. Dan didn't tell Cahir until it was an accomplished fact. He said he wanted to work for the year, save a bit of money, and he ventured no excuse beyond that. Cahir thinks it's normal to be scared.

Whatever the reason, it wasn't what Mum and Dad wanted to hear. Graham and Marie had their big plans, their trip of a lifetime, organised to fit with Dan's removal over the water. And what? Were they going to cancel that? The county road engineer and the local enterprise officer had retired early and were off to examine the roads in South America. Off to report back on the exotic construction techniques of the southern hemisphere. You couldn't get in the way of that.

Marie sobbed when they were pulling out of the drive, heading for the airport bus. God, was she some terrible kind of mother to be going off like this? Cahir told her not to be worrying. The two adventurers had to be strong and get goodbye said because the boys were grown. Raised. They'd call, Marie said, as soon as they got to Panama.

Cahir is at the kitchen table with a book about the sixth mass extinction. In the same seat where he always did his homework; times tables and English comprehension and the islands, rivers and mountains of Ireland. The light comes from behind him, from the sunroom off the kitchen, filled with wicker furniture and pictures of a family holiday at the Mar Menor near Alicante.

Dan is making another round of toast, his skin pale against the shiny cabinets that Frankie Craig built and hung. Good solid units, untouched until Graham sprayed them a shimmering cream in 2004, the split cream shining and clashing with the yellow floor tiles, the same tiles they have in the Chinese takeaway beside the Park bar.

At the toaster, Bob Dylan is blaring out of Dan's phone. Normally Cahir doesn't like a lot of noise but Dan is so good at doing the voices. If you give him a few minutes to listen, he can recreate anybody. Cahir likes when he does Morrissey, Liam Gallagher and Alex Turner, but he likes Bob the most. It's so funny the face Dan pulls as he sticks out his chin and sings the nasally, gravelly verses.

36

Being with Dan in the house is the only thing better than being alone. Cahir can sit in front of Dan and not even want to fizz apart or disassemble. Learning to hold level took Cahir years of work. It was a tedious calibration process, experimenting with counting and predictability. The programming of a small, reliable set of functions. It was a regime of detachment and separateness, of not caring. He doesn't have to control what he doesn't care about.

At the high point of indignation, Dan sings furiously, demanding justice and thumping his foot on the tiles. His head bouncing, jerking at the sudden stops of the drums or the violin. A frontman with no band, drumming on his bare stomach and playing harmonica with a slice of toast. It's an unmoderated performance. Voice unrestrained. Hands flying. When there's nobody watching Dan is a big soft boy too and that's why Cahir will be able to show him the trees.

Cahir will show Dan the trees because Dan loves him. He knows for sure that Dan loves him because at his eighteenth birthday party, after everybody had left, Dan said he did, and even though Dan was drunk Cahir believed him. Elephant Ears doesn't forget the things that people say.

The trees will be like a gift for Dan and they'll belong to them both even if Dan is left the Yelper land because he'd never bar Cahir from working on it. Marie leaving the land to Dan is just the same as leaving it to Cahir. Once the leaves come out in the spring, when they're looking their best, Cahir will take Dan over and show him. When he's sure of what he has, he'll ask Dan to help. The new wood will outlast them both and it will be something to ask each other on the phone. Cahir knows people take better care of what they own and if he can make something perfect for Dan to own, something rooted in place, then Dan will have to keep coming home.

Tidying away the crumbs and washing the chocolate-smeared knife, Cahir tries hard not to lick the knife clean.

He is trying to feel brave. He is trying to be calm even though he is pushing past safe limits. Further into sway than he has gone before. There is a small tremble. There is a tiny shake but he is keeping steady. He is stood solid, humming at the sink.

The Big Shop

Saturday morning at the end of November and Dan is driving to work, down the Church Road on a provisional licence. His blood alcohol level is likely borderline but he drives on, lamps lit, into a hanging fog. Enda McMenamin says he's a grand driver, powerful clutch control, and he'll pass the test no bother after a couple more lessons. It's five o'clock in the morning and Dan had some trouble getting resurrected, he had a bit of trouble understanding the flashing numbers and songs, but he got himself up with the thought of Pup idling at the back gates. Bloody fucking Pup is never late.

There was no time to clean up. The pool of vomit at his bedpost suggests that none of it was dreaming. Dan was full and then he was emptied. A few rolling heaves and a big messy spill. He hadn't time to shower but he brushed his teeth vigorously, and he washed his face and his neck three times in very cold water. He lashed himself with deodorant and picked a clean un-ironed T-shirt from the pile on the dresser.

Cahir might kill him for endangering the Starlet like this because she wouldn't take much of a bashing but there's nobody on the road at this hour and Dan's crawling. He screws down the window to let out wet air, to stick his head around the steamy windscreen, Cahir's old L-plates peeling at the corners, faded. Dan's sailing past the school at thirty-five miles an hour. She's revving at that speed and Dan could nearly try sticking her into fourth, not a bother on him.

Now that Dan is up, the worst might be over. He might be grand. He might maintain that hangovers are a state of mind and that he's only tired and his head is only ringing mental because the music was blaring all night. What else could he expect? It was a wild bit of noise. He'll have to find somewhere better to go. A rake of pints would be no bother if Dan could have them in a civil atmosphere. The air is fresh out the window. Cool and nice and fresh. Dan can't remember the meteorological difference between mist and fog but visually it reminds him of the dance floor in the Bailey, but better because of the quiet, even when his head is banging and nobody is looking to shift him.

In the empty car park under the hulking outline of the livestock mart, Dan is seven minutes late but all in one piece. He pops down the lock on the passenger side and sticks the key in his door. In fairness, she's some wagon. She's mint! Another couple of years and they'll qualify for vintage insurance.

Dan jogs to the side door, past the pharmacy and the crèche, comforted by the familiar and certain geometry of the retail units and the supermarket. In his current fragile state, the symmetrical assembly of shapes, the white render and huge regular sheets of glass, the flat silver roof with its bold, heavy edges, it's all a comfort to Dan. It's ambition. It's not a bit sorry. It's money and that's a solid thing to shelter under. The sharp edges of a commercial box are made to cut into the sky, to withstand it or ignore it.

Pup is waiting when Dan swings the back gate open.

Ah, sorry, Pup! I turned the fucking alarm off. Jesus Christ, I dunno, hi.

Pup turns to his work. He hasn't time for Dan's shit. The two of them work in silence, Pup rolling the cages off the embossed ramp of the lorry and Dan taking them from him, guiding them up beside the cardboard compacter, shuffling backwards ahead of their momentum and watching for wonky wheels. Washing powder tablets and toilet roll. Pet food and shampoo. Biscuits, nut butters, peas and beans and protein bars.

Dan tries to arrange the delivery by category so it's easier to unpack. He knows how annoying it is when you have to keep moving back and forth between *Take Home Confectionery* and *Ethnic Sauces*. Dan doesn't have to pack anything now. He can leave the big cages there in lines until Dermot and Lucy and Rebecca come in. You need cooperation in a big shop, for packing orders, and doing stock takes, and burden-sharing on the rota so that everybody gets the hours that suit them. There's a lot to be done, and

41

more than there might be, because some of the others are clean useless.

Have you the return cages tied up? asks Pup.

Should be, aye, says Dan.

He hopes to God they are. Was it Michael working yesterday? He hopes it was Michael. Not Hugh anyway. A fucking tube. Hugh is an insult to tubes. Dan potters around with the new cages, spinning them neat beside each other and wondering how Hugh can be so useless until Pup comes back to him with the handheld device, holding up the screen for Dan to sign, his name flowing thick and smudging from the plastic pen. As the lorry pulls out of the yard and Dan swings the gates closed, the day is slipping in and it's worse Dan's getting. In twenty minutes he could plausibly be as far on so he leaves Aine and Jeanette to the baking and slopes up the back stairs to the canteen. He doesn't bother with the lights, just drums his fingers along the white walls for orientation, lightly, so he doesn't pull down the food safety charts. When you're cooking, 5 to 63 degrees Celsius is the danger zone. That was part of his induction training as a high-risk food handler. In the canteen Dan puts on the kettle and stands at the sink, wiping the counters with a disposable yellow cloth while he waits. The square window at the sink looks over the metal roof and up to chimney pots around the Diamond. He can see the top of Sliabh Sneacht under the moon and the cross on the dome of the church is shining. It'll be a good bright day when the sun gets up and the first sip of coffee is a help to him, rinsing his mouth of leftover mint.

*

It was late when they managed to get drunk, after eleven when the last of the egg and onion sandwiches were moved to the kitchen. Sarah Charlis was eighteen and the party was in a white marquee tied on to the shed. Time was against them so they played a game of cards where all the suits were bad news and Dan had to swallow a horrible cup they kept in the middle and filled gradually with splashes of vodka, pear cider, Guinness, and gin. He sank it when the time came because they all cheered and he even kept it down for a few hours, good man himself, drinking like he was making a point, hoping he'd surprise them with the nerve required. The room swam for a minute but Dan found his way to the kitchen, for another few sandwiches, hoping they would stand to him in some way. On his way back, Sarah and her mum caught him in the hall and Sarah's mum asked him what he was going to do on this year out of his? And he told her he was going to learn the tuba because he is a total dick.

The tuba? she asked.

Aye, Dan said, his arm around Sarah's neck. It's a vocation, Eileen. A solemn calling. You just don't say no to the Carndonagh Brass Band, Eileen. You don't. And you know, there's like a yearning in my soul for this kind of thing. You couldn't miss it. The yearning. The big tuba boom.

Eileen laughed as he mimed embrace and puffing effort, holding his breath until he went red. She was close to flirting with him as he explained that the danger of a musical regret is that you'll never get it out of your head. You'd be haunted by a jingle unlearned.

Sarah led him away eventually, holding his arm where it

43

came out from under his short sleeves and Dan thought, yeah, I would shift Sarah.

Hello? Keyarn Cabs?

They shouted to the poor man as they got into the taxi and then shouted at him as they got out.

It's a scandal, they squealed. It's a money racket! Thank God they didn't mention your man's mullet. Inside the nightclub, there was nothing but roaring and sickening shots.

A troupe of bare-bellied girls in tight bands, top and bottom, walked past them hand-in-hand like baby shrews, only surviving as a collective. Amy at the back, electric and brave, cleaved off to hug Dan. Her backcombed hair was like a blonde mist around her head, her skin was white in the UV light and the swivelling beams. White skin covered in layers and layers of white fabric, all slight on their own, the wisps were gradually heavy enough to cover some of her but not any of what mattered to Dan. They were falling at the same rate, the two of them winners in a place like this. Ready to whisper, Amy stood close until Dan stopped thinking. Until restless hands strangled wit and censors were stomped flat by instinct and want. Further over the hall, in a crook of a shelf opposite the Ladies toilet, Amy opened her arms for Dan and he stepped in kissing her, their hands at each other's face, his dick stiff at her hip, smiling at each other but never breaking fully apart. The world spinning for both of them until the lights lifted and the National Anthem started. They walked to the chip van then, holding hands so everybody saw they were shifting. Dan bought her a curry cheesy chip and two battered sausages with his last tenner. One sausage for her and one for him and they sat on the kerb with a coat over her shoulders, stooping over the heat of her champagne Styrofoam box, Amy carefully spooning curry sauce into her mouth in the dark. Dan threw half of a sausage back into the yellow box and walked off alone, down Pound Street without a word, flushed orange under the street lamps and tortured with the noise of the Honda Civics. When Dan got home he puked all over the far side of the bed.

At the sink, Dan can feel himself floating off with egg and onion rising in his sinuses, but he can grasp at the danger zone which is between 5 and 63 degrees. It's nice that some things are definitely true. Dan got an award for science after his Junior Cert because that's the social engineering Santa can manage when he brings you a chemistry set three years in a row and your own Bunsen burner before you're really fit to tinker with an open flame. Shorthand names like Science Boy are grand for a while but lately Dan has had a rethink. Amy the Rye wouldn't have had any interest in skinny Science Boy. She likes his hair and his big arms. That's why you have to be a bit callous and get the strangling done. You have to make yourself from scratch. Search for a picture you like and recreate it. Bin the previous iterations. Being self-made is easier if you have a good head for lies, for stories to help you with the cover-up and to explain why it wasn't even bad at all. It's lucky for Dan that him and Cahir were brought up on fictional heroes.

The boys like the same funny thoughts. The same jokes and stories. Dan tells Cahir what goes on at the shop. About the different characters. The different intrigues. Who's not talking to who in the canteen. The wee dramas of an evening shift like when Dan was conned by the tanned girl with her tits hanging out. Or about the different ways people buy drink. Shifty, with a shake in their hand at half ten in the morning. Just a few cans of IPA for starters. So tart it's as good as breakfast juice.

He tells Cahir who won what on the Lotto or on the Telly Bingo. Who had a horse or a dog or a team come in at big odds. About the online order that was just twenty bottles of beer and two Cadbury's Freddos. About your man in buying half a loaf, instant coffee and two Diamond Doublers. Laughing. All the time laughing. Only talking in the middle of laughing. Him and the wife play the Diamond Doublers, but the luck's run out. No luck any more. Laughing because nothing ever changes. Laughing because we're all just wind-up toys. Wind us up and off we go.

Coming across the smooth, speckled resin floor, summoning a firmer grip on specifics, Dan basks in the general coolness of the air, chilled by the fridges and freezers, feeling very lightly refrigerated. He walks the wide aisles and lets his eyes adjust to the golden light. The mix of daylight and warm white, distributed by an expensive system of spots and panels and pendants, arranged so that fake oak and wicker baskets glow in the bakery, so that stainless steel and crushed ice gleam in the fishmonger's, so that butchered flesh looks more pink and piled apples look more green. The temperatures and smells are all sifted by a network of mechanical ventilation and heat recovery so that you can comfortably browse the varied produce of the earth. Picked, shipped, flown, trucked, and packed in neat formation. Lit and priced for sale. The logos on the cans and bags are arranged in towers and baskets for overwhelming effect. Thousands and thousands of lines. It's the romance of a well-run supermarket that they're trained to love you whoever you pretend to be, where personable cashiers will talk their might and let you graze them with your fingertips as long as you're handing over money. Some of them are born naturals turning polite distance to its best commercial return.

Dan lifts his head in time to meet Bernard Glen coming to the first berry fridge; blueberries and raspberries, blackberries and strawberries stacked higher than the recommended load line. Bernard is the big boss man. He took over a corner shop from his dad and now he owns half of Derry City. Houses upon houses. A casino at the border and pubs galore. They say it's the wife that's the brains of the operation. The balls too. That Anne was from some big family of shirt makers in Belfast and that snaring her was Bernard's smartest move. Bernard is getting stuck into date rotation. He can afford to faff about with turnips and ginger roots because he has his money made long ago. And because he's got his son John installed. Just recently, the next generation tied in to full operational control. That leaves Bernard the time to chat, to court, to strategise, to grant small waves and favours as he passes, believing in success completely, like the local boy who became bishop or a cabinet minister. John Glen, that's Bernard's son, he's a sound fella. Dan gets on the best with him. He's learning quick since he came back from the Far East and he generally chats sense. Like how it's a scandal what Glengad and Aileach are getting away with in the Inishowen League. John's a solid character. Very even mannered no matter who he's talking to. All the bread men and merchandisers are treated equal. Cahir says John wasn't serious about staying away because rich people always act to protect the nucleus of their wealth. Cahir says John is a nasty prick who shouldn't get away with any of it. He says he's a sinecurist and that inherited wealth is a poison that can only be neutralised by nationalisation and redistribution. Cahir likes to use big words when talking about people he dislikes. He pronounces them with special emphasis and often with difficulty. Dan mostly knows the words already. He often knows the correct pronunciation but he wouldn't bother correcting Cahir.

As the only heir of a small merchant fortune, Dan admits John would be vulnerable to a well-planned execution. Then Dan could come back from the trainee manager programme with a compelling case for a takeover. A safe pair of hands for a tired man's legacy. Being honest, Bernard doesn't look too tired. Coming down past the berry fridge in his pink shirt and navy slacks, he's ready for work like he always was.

Dan puts out the newspapers first, cutting the cords and marking off quantities, flipping the bundles so the titles face out. He arranges them by format and market segment.

Redtops. Compact dailies. Broadsheets. He puts the coffee machine on to rinse, refills the grinder and then stands at the till until teatime, tidying confectionery and taking money for cappuccinos and multipack Mars bars and packets of Benson and Hedges. Some of the men's hands are dusty from yesterday and dry-looking. Carn is famous for plasterers. It's the town trade and nobody does it better. Like in the Renaissance when some towns specialised in a craft. In the use of one material or mix. The men in Carn, they coat bricks in smooth finish. Daub walls with a hawk and trowel. Scratch coats and rubbing up and skim. A hard veneer and sometimes a cornice. Cob. Gypsum. Lime. Cement. Trying to create a bit of neatness, a bit of order like men always have. And they head off in groups, in the back of Transit vans, men who will throw up gauges of plaster until their back or shoulders give way. Some of them don't want to chat. Some of them are furious. It takes a toll on a labourer, remaking the earth like that. Heaving the jackhammered rubble, squinting in the dust. No masks, no gloves to stop their hands going floury, the dust sucking the moisture out of them. Sand and cement dust absorbing what is living in you.

After them come the office workers and the teachers and though it's a luxury to be on the road after eight, you wouldn't know it from the faces on them. They don't see the civilisation in their time of rising. They don't see the raw faces on the boys in at half-six, sleepwalking toward a tight siege of work on the sites, undaunted when Dan checks their EuroMillions ticket and tells them, It's not a winner, sorry. You may head up the road.

Give me two lines for tomorrow night's Lotto and twenty purple Silk Cut, says Benny Tourish. He hands Dan a sandwich wrapped in brown greaseproof paper and lifts a large takeaway cup to catch Dan's eye.

Tea in that, Benny says.

Benny's sandwich is always the same: one sausage, two bacon, and a hash brown. White bread, red sauce and butter. The bread is halved straight down the middle and Benny is particular about that because he says the sausage falls out if you cut it into triangles.

At ten o'clock Phelim McCloskey asks Dan did he see the match? Dan can't think what match Phelim means. He's normally good with that kind of thing but it's a challenge when he's trying not to breathe. Phelim stinks. Nothing to do with his own odours. It's the smell of fish too long out of the water. Occupational. The smell of the factory isn't handy chased off a boiler suit, so Dan tries hard to smile the normal amount. A man deserves civility when he's buying a jumbo sausage roll in the morning.

The rugby, was it? Dan asks.

Phelim looks at Dan like he's a dum-dum. He picks up his snack pack of bananas with a scowl, crabbit before tea-time, like it's a penance to be speaking.

I wouldn't watch that tripe, Phelim says. The football, I mean.

Phelim is a soccer man and Dan should have known that.

I didn't actually see it, Phelim, Dan says, and then the two of them wait for the receipt, not a peep between them, eyes on the printer with no chance of recovery. Jesus, Phelim is fucking ruthless, moving off in silence, fixing up his stinking suit and flattening his twenty-euro note in beside the others. There's plenty of money in the crabs but even if there wasn't you can't turn your nose up at honest work. Dan feels safe believing that now. He's just as honest in his work as Phelim and the plasterers when he's mopping the public toilets and sorting shelf edge labels by hand. Everyday duty is a great thing to know about, one of many things Dan has learned around the shop. Matas, for example, the Polish lad in snazzy sneakers, he taught Dan how to build giant sawtooth displays of cereal boxes and towers of multipack Coke cans that interlock and shine out in sugared red. Matas is always running around shouting at whoever fucked up the price-checking. That's his value to the Glens. Dan once heard Bernard Glen say to him,

It's all about the numbers, Matas.

Sales less Cost of Sales is probably what Bernard means. Or maybe he was talking about gap reports, or weekly waste percentages or underlying margins. They're always top in the region anyway and that's on account of Matas and the numbers he contends with. They're winners in a beautiful set. It really is top class. Millions were borrowed and spent so that it could be sparkling clean but full of warm colours and rustic shopfitting. They're a cast of bodies that come and go, extras amid the principals, all with an adopted role, a tone and script to fit the story of service.

We go the extra mile to earn your smile.

A few have gathered by the newspaper stand and they're not smiling. They're waiting for Dan to ask, Who's next there?

*

Is he stupid or something?

That's what Breda McColgan wanted to know. It's four medium Soft Batch Rolls for two euro and Dan charged her for Demi-Baguettes! Which are sixty-three cents each! What kind of stupid fucker can't separate a Demi-Baguette from a medium Soft Batch Roll? See, Dan was trying to give Breda a summary of the recent political upheaval in the UK, pacing himself for completeness. If he had known she only wanted to be charged correctly for her bread rolls he would have been grand. With such a serious quantity of knowledge to be accumulated, the road to mastery involves a lot of mis-sold baked goods. Pain au chocolat, vanilla cream Danish, maple pecan plait, Portuguese custard tarts. Dan didn't know one from the other and he was very slow with the change too. It's hard at first to get the right coins from the right slots and think of a parting remark. What he learned early on, after the Demi-Baguette debacle, is that there's great escape in prophecy. You can dole one out to everybody without fear.

Did you hear what they're giving?

It's to be worse tomorrow!

Accuracy is irrelevant, it's the reprieve you need, so you have time to sort the coppers. Actually, Dan's not stupid. He's a classic stew. Top of the class and all that. The height of glory for the son of two civil servants.

The day of his Leaving Cert results, Dan was pier-jumping in Culdaff. Marie picked up his certificate from the school and Cahir came looking for him. It was a really hot day and none of the boys were interested in their results. There was a terrible fear on them from the night before so they got a few orange Calippos and some Loop the Loops and went to the water. Oisín and Rory were going to do shit anyway and Dan wasn't going to the school by himself to stand and take pictures with Mr Mullins. Bunagee was busy with cars because a group of dolphins had been performing offshore for the previous week but Dan and Oisín and Rory were the only bodies getting wet. They had been diving for an hour or so when the Starlet pulled on to the pier. It was Rory that spotted Cahir.

I know that banger, he said, splashing water over Dan and jumping on to Dan's shoulders trying to push him underwater. You must have failed everything you dunce.

Cahir's car did look funny beside Rory's A3 because the Starlet is from 1997 and has so many dings and bashes it looks like it was hammered by hand from a lump of pliable tin. Rory's Audi is very handy for Dan because he doesn't have his full licence yet and because Cahir normally refuses to drive anywhere. If Cahir sees Rory's car pulling in at the house he normally makes some remark about the spoils of ecocide or about Rory's parents scavenging among the ruins of late capitalism.

When Dan climbed from the water Cahir was giddy. He obviously knew already.

Well?

Dan hardly had to guess. The smile on Cahir's face was deforming, it was that wide. He was stretched with happiness. His face and his whole body were bursting into weird shapes as he tried to embody it. He went to hand Dan the brown envelope.

Not a bit of it, said Dan. You read them to me, I'm all wet.

Cahir tore open the envelope seal and pulled out the stiff sheet of paper. He came round to Dan's side and held it in front of them both. Then he ran his finger down the right-hand side of the page. Six As and one B.

Dan was happy that Cahir was happy. It was Cahir's achievement as much as his own. Cahir never stopped hounding Dan about study. They more or less studied together, Cahir sitting in the room beside him, relearning the verbs himself, writing out little summary cards and composing tests.

Not bad, ha?

Pretty good yeah, said Cahir.

Dan clapped him on the shoulder and told him to take the certificate home. I'll see yous for dinner, he said. Dan turned back to the sea, took a big run-up and threw himself into the air, hugging his legs to his chest and bombing deep into the water.

A year out, is it?

And what, work in the shop, is it?

One year. One and that's it. No more than a year or you'll be stuck. Cahir is always very clear about that.

Dan fetches his lunchbox from his locker at teatime. If he was the sort who got hangovers he'd be sick as a dog. At the hot food counter the chicken tenders are tempting. Dry-looking. The jambons are soggy and he can tell they're damp underneath. Dan thinks about Cahir coming down for his lunch. He'll be furious because the wedges are finished. If there's no wedges Cahir always gets a sausage and a croissant in separate bags and then makes himself a butty with taco sauce. He pretends he doesn't like sausages. He thinks Dan doesn't see him stuff it in. Aine puts a southern fried chicken fillet in Dan's tin box and he jogs up the back stairs. He'll leave it off his food log for the gym. Dan is fading now. Holy God he's fading and Jesus bastarding Christ. Ah, come on. Come on now and look at him. Wrecked and starved. His face swollen. Hair shite. Blue aftershock and sweat pouring out of him.

Dan is standing outside the canteen door looking through the slit window. He already clocked out so he can't go back down to the floor and what if Lydia looks up from her magazine and her low-fat vanilla yoghurt with real chocolate sprinkles? He's standing staring at her through the window and all he can think is that it costs eighty-six cents, that yoghurt. He can't stand at the window staring in at her and Kathleen McGrenra. He is stuck on the spot until he hears steps on the back stairs. He walks back up the hall and reapproaches the door as John Glen rounds the corner and makes one of those smiles that hold no emotion, only an effort of his facial muscles. John has nice stubble and he looks fresh.

How's John?

Not too bad, Dan. Busy down there th'day, ha? John opens the door and Dan walks in smiling at Lydia. A big uncool goofy smile. He may as well fall prone at her feet.

Yes Lydia, says John. It's a typical local greeting. It's how he operates. John keeps all the staff on good terms but not personal terms. Dan sometimes wonders if John enjoys his work. When things are busy he doesn't chat. When he's physically exerting himself, he can't do small talk. Bernie John-Eddie says it's 'cause he's not used to the hard graft. Gertie the Coiner says it's 'cause he's too superior. Too important to talk to them down in the off-licence. But old Gary Crossan, the butcher, he says that's nonsense. That the work is bred into him. The ethic and fear. That he was at his dad's side every day when he was a boy. His father's son.

Dan's own leg is bouncing but he's cool. He's a cool man. A handsome man should be able to stand still and act like an ordinary human. John doesn't have a jawline under his stubble and look at him. Very calm. While John is getting a mug from the cupboard, Dan dumps his spicy chicken fillet in the bin and checks his hair in the chrome of the water boiler. In the same movement as reaching for the milk, he runs his hand through his fringe, hoping for camouflage.

Do any of you need tea? John asks Lydia and Kathleen.

No thanks, Lydia says.

She's so polite. Dan leaves his empty lunchbox in the fridge and sits at the table with a strong cup of tea and his phone. Lydia keeps her hair in a knot and files escapee strands behind her ears. So swish in faded black it hardly looks like the uniform at all. Her teaspoon shines out over the plastic yogurt pot, held in her slim fingers like a weapon that's both fundamental and refined.

John is stirring his cup at the sink. Smiling at whatever is in his emails, or his calendar, or his bank account. He's bulky but not fat. They say he's very fit now since he got mad into the cycling and you'd have to agree he's quite tasteful for a businessman, like, there's no pinstripes or anything. Dan is trying to read Lydia's magazine from across the table. An article about a man who builds chairs. He is trying to understand what she loves about a furniture maker.

Holy Mary Mother of God she is going to eat a cream bun. That's indecent. Dan, you dirty fucker, leering at the poor girl and her wee treat. Her fat treat sitting on a napkin beside her banana skin and her rice cake. McDaid's Bakery know their way around a cream bun. That's for sure. Dan sometimes signs their delivery docket in the morning, counting them out, lined on to the baking parchment, turning it translucent with the surplus oil that runs from their pores; chocolate Gravy Rings, Coconut Snowballs, Turnovers and Blockings. Cream Fingers with slicks of shiny cream and squirts of ruby jam in the cleft, the whole length powdered with sugar.

Lydia eats so slowly. Dan loves that. Watching her, he realises that he's a sloppy eater. Too desperate. Look at this! She hasn't a clue about desperation. Look at her eating so slow. There's self-control in that. Lydia chews so many times because she is so well brought up. Dan is close to counting them for his own record. She isn't getting it all in her mouth though. How can she be so classy with sweet cream stuck under her nose? She's like the fucking aristocracy. It's her straight nose and her cheekbones and her big sad eyes. She cleans the edges of her lips. Dan's phone has gone dark from inactivity. John is heading out the door but before he gets there he turns back and asks Lydia would she go to Moville and pick up the lodgements for him, he doesn't think he'll have time today.

Lydia looks up and shrugs. Yeah, no bother, she says.

John sees the cream on her face. A big smile breaks out in him. He looks like he's going to say something, but then he stops, irons out his smile. OK, great, he says. Thanks. The door closes gently after him.

Lydia looks back at Dan. What's he laughing at? What's so funny?

Your bun, Dan says. It's all over your face.

She's wile bold then. Full of the devil as she scrapes the cream on to her finger, throwing the last bit of bun into her mouth, dissolving it.

I don't know what yous are all gawking at. We're still allowed to eat cream buns, you know. We're not all on hunger strike, she says, nodding down at Dan's empty place. She throws her yogurt pot in the bin and pushes a lock of hair behind her ears. I'm going to get an eating disorder now, she says, and that'll show yous. Do you hear that, Kathleen?

John is gone but Dan and Kathleen and Lydia laugh together and Lydia catches Dan's eye over the distance she normally keeps and there's conspiracy in how close she lets him. She leaves the air in agitation but the table tidy, no physical proof of her left in the room. Kathleen is back at her crossword and Dan sits on in silence. He sips his tea happy that he doesn't have to go back on the till because Mary Mullier started there at twelve and he'll tip away at the ambient aisles and pack the big minerals until he can go over the hall to the Good As New shop. To Cahir's room full of previously owned shirts and funny lamps. In the corner of the building above and apart from the hustle of the supermarket floor below, it'll be an afternoon easy spent, sleeping in the good green velvet chair, quiet watching the weather on Trabrega Bay.

Trespass

It is a different world in the global south. So says Graham in his latest dispatch. So many people, he says. The cities are hard to believe, they stretch so far. The two of them are eaten alive with the mosquitos and even though nobody else is taking their antimalarials, Marie is sticking to her prescription rigorously. They found this black soap that the American military developed, and they rub it dry on to their skin in a thick coat. Without it they'd never have made it through the Colombian jungle. There were two wee cutties from Sweden and the legs on them when they came out, not a patch spared. Red and swollen all over with the tiny sores.

Since then they've been in the mountains. They've been staying with an Australian man and his pet goats on a ranch at the base of Cotopaxi; a volcano that looks just like Mt Fuji but that's very easy to get photos of. Their host drove them as far as the snow line. Five thousand metres above the sea and they hardly had to walk at all. Next week they are going to the Galapagos to see all the birds and then they have a river cruise in the Amazon. Marie wondered if Cahir has ever heard of ayahuasca?

Cahir listens to the excerpts that Marie reads to him from her travel diary and hopes there isn't a part about the bodily truths she learned while on jungle acid. Cahir thinks repression must be worth something if it stops you shitting secrets at a shaman's feet.

He is washing bottle tops in the staff toilet. The bits and pieces he gleaned from Kinnagoe Bay. The smell of the lids isn't great, a mix of sour milk and stale beer. Cahir wants to make something from the waste blown ashore. Since he got the trees started, new ambition rises for all his efforts. Even for the Good As New.

Cahir's shop is upstairs, above the supermarket, in the top corner of the structure where glass walls meet. The metal clothes rails are set out on bare concrete slabs and the wooden shelves are nailed to unplastered walls. The roof is held up by white powder-coated beams and pillars, veined in red wires that run from the sprinklers and sounders of the fire alarm. Two of the four walls are made of glass, tinted a little blue and divided by heavy grey frames. The glass and the height make for a great lookout. A perch or crow's nest. Cahir can spot all approaching hazards, for example, customers. Cahir hates to see customers coming but he knows that if he's polite and quiet, they'll leave soon enough and he can put everything back in its right place. From the perch, Cahir can look into the gardens across the road and watch the car park entrance. He can watch the traffic on the Malin Road and the shifting light on the high jaws of Trabrega Bay.

He bought a silver sparrow from a boy in Letterkenny and hung it above the door of the shop. It's his only decoration and he doesn't jingle. He's not supposed to. He's just proof that shitty broken things can be put back together. That there's a future for discarded parts that are not inherently defective or poorly made, just finished with or forgotten. It's a lovely piece of work, the lids hammered flat, pierced, folded and sewn together so that the clean metal faces out. An armoured sparrow hanging over the door, poised and light. Cahir's already planning the things he can whittle from forest thinnings. Waste wood will be his preferred medium. At Christmas he'll make baubles, paint them gold and red and green, and sell them at the markets or downstairs next to the chocolate reindeers. See, the glamour of the revolution may be painted on dead bodies but there's a lot of work goes into it before that. Going up the stairs, the washed lids rattle like seashells in the box.

The stuff they bring him isn't as good as new. It's mostly rubbish. Scratched DVDs and books with tattered jackets and broken plastic toys. Teddies they got in a Happy Meal. The odd board game or jigsaw. Cahir has a very cool collection of games and puzzles. Underrated, he thinks. The majority is clutter really, and Cahir doesn't keep it all. You have to pick what you think can survive, what shouldn't be chucked yet. Cahir sorts through the curios, the delft and knick-knacks, comedy mugs and lamps that look like parrots. He distinguishes glass and crystal and has learned to hear the telltale musical ring, to feel the weight of high lead content. Dan tells him what clothes to keep, the shirts and blouses that are worth ablution, worth setting on display. What scarves and neckties to hang on the clothesline, strung between the metal rails.

Cahir pays attention to the ventilation of the space, to neutralising must with lemon juice and baking soda and he has a few potted plants dotted about to filter the air. Ferns and spider plants in mismatched pots on his desk and on the windowsills.

For the bother of it, he takes a small wage but all other proceeds are for charity. He has a list of the beneficiaries stuck up behind his desk: the Galway Cancer Bus, the Colgan Hall, Lifeline Inishowen. There is no end of worthy causes. Cahir thought he could do no harm, opt out, but in the avalanche of waste, in the bags and bags they kept bringing, he saw that it would never be enough. He had to create good, not just wash and organise what was bad.

Dan won't be here until two o'clock. Cahir wants to casually mention something he read about Thomas Aquinas. It's harder than you think to find a natural time to mention Thomas Aquinas. Self-directed learning is tricky that way. They've nobody to guide or censure them. Nobody to check if they've done the recommended reading. Like they're freshers in a badly run college, scrolling their phones and telling each other every new thing they come across. Asking each other to explain whatever made them laugh or curse or sigh. Good As New wisdom all around. Cahir didn't go to college but that was no excuse for stupidity. He doesn't think Dan's year out should mean nothing learned. A bit of learning is the minimum required so that the boys'll not go spaltering into the world unformed. With ascetic habits and the money their mum and dad send for house-keeping, they're a small burden on the state. It's not dodgy or anything. They're no cowboys. The log of days worked and not worked is written out accurately. Cahir fills the forms for the both of them. He makes sure the Xs and Os are in the right place.

It's only just noon so Cahir has plenty of time to be away to Carrick and back by two. Tuesday afternoons are famously shit for footfall and he has been thinking about how dusty the birch stems looked. How crispy the buds felt and how it could be a stillborn grove, them all dead in their holes while he gloats. He takes a penknife from the shelf, removing the string and the little price tag. It's a single blade with a mother-of-pearl handle, a leather tassel hanging from the loop end. He's going to perform a scratch test. He's going to scrape a piece of bark from the trunk to look for signs of sap, for vital green running under the skin.

It's sunny out but the wind would skin a cat. It's that easterly wind, his mum would say. Forcing him to take pleasure in his coat and the light at the edge of the lane. The narrow trail to the little wood. The quality of the light is colder, lower and it holds things in clarity, leaving them perfectly themselves every way he turns his head. There are no smudges he would make, no tidying necessary. Nothing to fix or ignore or keep out of sight. Nothing to ruin his idea of a place. It's a walk in diminishing light. The days are shorter and shorter. Daylight will soon be an aberration. Cahir tries harder to see it. Soak in it. Keep his eyes open as wide as he can. Expose his skin to the disappearing light. He greedily watches the colours in the sky. The chilled, stretched out, faded colours. They have to last him through winter and a long spell of artificial brightness in the shop.

Soon, a clear day like this will bring a hard frost to the hedgerow trees and vines, to the grass growing up the middle of the stone track. Not yet. Cahir walks very slow up the lane, basking in the cold slanting light. At the end of the path, to either side of the rusted iron gate, fuchsia bushes wriggle woody stems through the wire fence, hanging and dripping their red and purple skirts to rot in and among the ferns. Nothing is wrong until he gets to the flaking orange gate, to their marks in the brown slop.

For once Cahir wishes he was wrong. That they weren't broken in, slopping in and around the trees, their careless hooves on his cathedral floor. Panic chokes his sinuses, hot and wet like puke, blinding him to anything but the surge as he stands there.

For fuck's sake.

Jesus Christ. God, for fuck's sake. Cahir is comfortable addressing God, like all good boys who know the words at Mass by heart. He pleads with God to help him and to exist now that Cahir needs a hand. He bargains freedom, he scans his heart for bondage, anything good enough to sacrifice. The herd has turned the high part of the field to muck. Tramped and shit all over it. Huge wet pools of shit without skin. Fresh shit and destruction. Every minute they're in there is a minute they could kill him. They can trample him, rip the trees out with big curling tongues and straight hard teeth. He gets up on the bottom rung of the gate swinging his leg over and down shakily into a deep print so the brown water splashes up into his sock. He is watching them and they are watching him too. Sixteen suckler cows in shades of black and brown. One of them shuffles at the noise of the splash but Cahir stands still, urging calm. At least until he figures out how to move them. He takes the penknife from his pocket, like he could defend himself. He can see the two birches, tall as his shoulder, standing up. He edges toward them, his arms stretched out for balance between the dry tufts and in offering. He reaches the tips of his fingers and gently strokes the first stem. Everything isn't over. Some of them are still munching. Swinging their tails, moving along slowly, chomping and ripping with a brutal clip, squishing in the muck. Cahir is in the middle of them now. Powerless beside them because fury is nothing when they have the numbers. They can't understand his anger and they know no reason to fear him. Cahir says, HUP! like he heard farmers shout but they don't move. Stupid, fat, lazy cows so greedy they couldn't stay in their own fucking field. So stupid they can't even tell what's holy. Why can't they just fuck off?

He steps across the slope trying to spot the other trees. The biggest oak is under that brown one, coming up to her belly, whole and unbroken. She doesn't know it's there or she doesn't hate him. God doesn't hate him. The big girls are still clipping, munching, ripping the rushes and tufts. Cahir keeps moving. He bends to be sure of the smallest oak. There is no God again.

In the middle of the copse, Cahir stops, looking at them again. They're looking back with wet, cartoonish eyes, coquettishly batting them like pretty girls who know their luck. How do you move on from a sixteen cow stand-off? They are moaning. One of them is bellowing. Calling to the others. Or to him. Dripping a sticky stream of saliva. Too thick to fall away clean, it hangs like a bubbly thread, a mucosal strand of pure light hanging in the air, catching what wind there is and floating in it, anchored to her slick flopping gums. He rubs his eyes and takes a big breath of cold air, then makes a small start toward them. He needs to drive them on. They are cows. They are used to being driven. The first few scramble but resettle. The others don't flinch. The biggest brown cow is closest to him now, chopping at the earth, sniffing her way along, slapping her feet into the wet puddles, coming to him. Her bony legs getting splashed with dirty water. She stops moving and bellowing, stops munching and clipping. In the silence of them all standing still, looking away, she starts pissing. A sudden gushing drop of piss-yellow-piss. Cahir jumps back from the spray, stumbling in another puddle. She's got spirit. The arrogance that comes from huge haunches. The piss keeps gushing, spattering the wet soil immodestly and she stares at Cahir straight on, steaming from wet pink nostrils. Then bending her head, taking her glassy eyes away from him, she grabs the smallest oak, just the tip of it in the curl of her tongue is enough to pull it from the ground. Cahir groans and stumbles toward her in the uneven, trodden muck, swiping his blade into the air like he would cut her. It isn't the noise that chases her, it's an attack. They are all running, forgetting their power and the ease with which they could stay. They share her fear and get moving, skipping, and the noise is a horrible wet clatter. Cahir goes after them, stamping wherever he has to, soaked already, following them until they're through the gap into the next field. Run out the gap they came in. She spat it out in front of him so it wasn't any use to her. She couldn't even eat it. Spat chewed, split stems frayed from her teeth.

Cahir moves through the rushes, bowed by the sway of their bellies, bent and flattened where they had been lying, like the makings of a woven mat. He shoves the wee tree back in its hole of course, he firms the soil in, holding the stem in place and he runs to the pump at the road with his can, covered in muck, risking exposure on a Tuesday lunchtime when the school bells are ringing, and it might be too late already.

Cahir stands at the new clearing, staring at them, hoping they remember his intention and his knife. Staring at the posts wedged aside by their sloppy caravan as it pushed between the hedgerow gorse. Cahir needs a sharper barrier. He needs a real deterrent. Something to seal a slit that's too wide for stitches. He needs packing. The stones lying about are all too small and there isn't time to assemble them, or chip them so they rest steadily on each other, but mountains can be made of other things and Cahir can move them with what's coursing in his body. He won't have nothing again.

He goes to the dried out fossils, the heaps of dry, rotting scrub and he starts to pull them apart, catching the ends of the old trunks and briars and boughs to see what might come loose and what might come tumbling after, dragging the great ragged shapes down the field one by one and setting them between the holly tree and the barbed fence above the stream. Angling them in against the gorse, against posts in the fence, into the muck. Stacking trunk on trunk and branches on top, trying to spike them out and make them formidable. He pulls a full rowan tree from the pile, wiggling it until the dead roots slip free and dragging it to the gap to set behind the others, knitting and arranging it among the pricklier whins, hoping height, depth and thorn might make them rear like at a gruesome hurdle.

It's raining again and Cahir's hands are splintered and dirty from the soil, the dust, the moss on the old wood. To preserve the potential of the ground he'll need more than a makeshift dam. A patch job rarely lasts. It's much better to preserve the integrity of the original structure. Once a tear is made, even a very good sewing job won't cut it for long.

At home Dan left a note on the kitchen island: *You weren't at the shop so I locked up and went to Dermo's. Shop keys are in the letterbox. Be back Friday I'd say.*

It's a blessing to wash alone and cover up the small cuts on his hands in silence. Cahir can stand in his slippers in the clear night, trying to care about the constellations from a sheltered place in the garden, looking up into the darkness and letting the light come to his eyes over time.

Next morning, the air is cold and gusting and Cahir comes slowly to the gate, steeling for extinction, for complete loss. But it's all quiet. He had himself worked up for an ending but instead the work stretches out in front of him and the edges can't be seen. The dull grey sky hangs low to the ground, beheading high peaks. Everything is cold and even. The wind is penetrating his fleece, tunnelling up the lane from his right side and dull truth is all that's mustered when the light doesn't rise to trick him or throw a glare that can hint at hope. The puddles are everywhere, squelching on the poorly drained ground as his boots pull out of each dirty pucker. There was no new attack but the water is lying in their prints and at the base of the birch trunks. One of the hawthorns is looking black and the small oak must be in danger even though he can't see any sign of it on the smooth bark or on the crispy leaves. He can't believe his luck. That he has something so good all to himself. The forest above him sweeps across the hill, lit in places by a spark of auburn. It was a scare, a threat and he's proud of his response in sealing the enclosure, like the walls, thick and high around a wealthy city. Cahir bends and weeds a little more. He is solid, dreaming of manure and bigger fences and of winter once the cows are brought in. He wants a few different strands going, for resilience. He'll plant again before March, so the rotted, wilted, drowned or torn up will have new heads to hide under. That they might be salvaged under cover.

Choirmistress

Lydia would never have taken work in the shop if she had known John was coming home. If there had been any word of him leaving Hong Kong, she would have found something else. It was Dolly who arranged the job for her like she arranges everything.

Dolly had met Bernard Glen in the shop on a Friday, very innocent, in getting the messages, and Bernard said he was run off his feet. She was hardly looking for a few hours work was she? Dolly said that they had a good laugh and that he's a very civil man, Bernard Glen. Dolly just thought she might as well mention it. That Lydia was home and she might help them out. She was back this last three months and Dolly never saw so much brooding.

Lydia came in to work in the cash office. To count the money and mind the safe. When Veronica was sick in the summer, she even learned how to pay the wages and calculate a VAT return. There has been chat of sending her on a training course. So far, only chat. It's a very slight thread that links her to the work and that suits Lydia fine. She sits at her desk and she counts. She files and straightens. She reconciles the takings, notes discrepancies. She lodges the money and goes home.

It was some wake-up in September. Some jolt for a Monday morning. There was a meeting in the boardroom and they all crowded in. A new week for a new era and a new leader. Bernard and Fonsy, the store manager, stood at the far end of the room and announced Fonsy's retirement. They introduced John, who some of them probably remembered. John was home and he was taking over. He begged help and understanding. It'll take him a while, he said, to figure it all out and he'll need everyone rowing together, and they've a big task on their hands now, with the new Lidl in Buncrana. He was born and reared in this, he said. Since he was weighing spuds upstairs in the old shop on Malin Street. They're in it together and he can't wait to know them all.

John didn't look at Lydia but there were over fifty people jammed into the room. She had a new fringe and was wearing a shapeless sweater. Conor and Dan were probably blocking her. Maybe John didn't care whether she was there or not. It was a long time since school. Years since they had seen each other or spoken. Since Lydia left him for Belfast.

John gave her a quick hug when they did meet, a firm quick hug outside the cash office, so different to the hesitating way he used to touch her when they were teenagers. Lydia wanted to question him. How was he? What about

Hong Kong? She wanted to explain what happened to her and why she was back in Dolly's house. She would have said something to hint at how stupid she had been. To say she wasn't as stupid as that now. That she had learned a bit of sense, at least. That she had no idea he was coming back. She had been assured that he wasn't.

Lydia didn't get saying any of that because John broke away quick. He said it was great to see her. They would have to catch up sometime. Sorry to run but there was water leaking out of the rotisserie oven and the engineer wanted to talk to him. A big bill probably, he said.

They smile at each other as they pass in the hall, their faces momentarily bright but fading even as they say Hi! Mostly they don't meet at all and Lydia has got used to it as the end of a story. A steady drawn-out ending after a spike, a slow and measured ending with plenty of time to interrogate what led to it. It's what Lydia deserves.

Dolly was at Lydia to join the choir as soon as she came home. It would be good for her, Dolly said. Sure, didn't she always love singing?

In the kitchen of the Colgan Hall, under the stage, it's warm enough to sit comfortably if you keep your jacket on. The kitchen ceiling is high with steel tubes running over and down the walls, carrying wires to new pendant lights. There are old wooden sash windows and the wainscoting is painted light grey. The choir sits in semicircular rows radiating from Vera and her upright piano. Sopranos and altos on one side, tenors and bases on the other. It's a wholesome set-up. Like a big classroom of V-neck jumpers and sensible shoes. The women with their knees tight together. The men arguing over Latin pronunciations and time signatures, rowdy and jocular, pushing until Vera gets cross. They love her a bit cross. Singers sitting ready to learn. Asking Vera to play their line again, until they have it in their ear. Rasping, jittering, ringing clear, they thread and weave through each other, trying to match silences, louds and softs.

They made a big fuss of Lydia when she joined. A talented girl like her, they were fair going up in the world. Great to have a new face. A bit of vitality. A bit of vigour. The young men would be queuing up to get into the choir now. Turns out they weren't far wrong. The tenors have had to source an extra seat and John Glen is in the front row.

John is all change. In school, he was skinny and pale with a sideswept fringe. He wore bracelets made of leather plaits and wooden beads, like a surfer who had never been in the sun. On his cushioned seat, playing with his folder and talking to Paul the Saddler, John's hair is cut up short and he isn't wearing anything on his wrist, not even a watch. Sturdy in his heavy flannel shirt, he is prepared to sing. Lydia never once heard him sing. Even when he took up the bass guitar and played in Tony Carey's band, it was only an excuse to be in the pub. In every glance she allows herself, Lydia is looking for the boy she used to know. She thinks only his eyes are the same. His eyes and his freckles, the way the freckles spread over the bridge of his nose.

The scales are starting as Lydia and Dolly take their seats, humming up and down the octave, going higher and higher until they are stretching. Vera sings them their notes and plays the opening bars and the chords drift over the room like a deep breath, nudging them to start quietly.

She wants to know what John sounds like. She is on the point of telling Sheila McGinley to pipe down for once. Who knows what they would hear if she quietened her warble for once. During 'See, Amid the Winter's Snow', Lydia steals a peek. John is grave, sincere and eager for the rich sound coming clear from down his throat. Lydia has a dirty throb at the seriousness in his eyes. At the end of the phrase, he catches her and stops singing and they both look away.

The hazel fleck in John's eye is the same too. The flash in his eyes, like kindness. It's still there. John was kind to her when they were together, and Lydia enjoyed that at first.

Lydia remembers standing on the gravel path outside John's house, in the shadow cast by huge cedar trees. They were cold out of the sun and John had his hands in his pockets.

The trees marked the outer boundaries of the garden. They hid the house all year round. Higher than all the chimneys and the various peaks of the roof. Running in a great avenue from the gatehouse to the walled garden, over-grown and abandoned, to the tarmac tennis court, its net drooping, its wire fence loose from the posts.

A couple of times, when it was hot, they lay under the trees and read. John made cold drinks, stiff with whatever spirits were in the cabinet, and they listened to a mix of songs, happy sunshine music and sad jazzy singers. Lydia drifting away with their voices. Unable to concentrate on the words in her book, convinced, converted by whatever the voices meant. Lydia would sing too and John said nobody could sing like her. That she made everything seem true. One more, he would say. Go on. Please.

Standing in the cold on the gravel path, none of it was enough. Lydia didn't want it any more. Not the way the grass was coming up through the tennis court. Not the rough bark on the trees. Not even a good Carn man like John.

Lydia always thought she could make John do anything, that he was willing at her fingers, but it wasn't quite true and she would rather burst than have a future settled at eighteen. When John and his dad talked about his future, they said *when*, not *if*. A life tied to daddy's plan and not a question asked. John was going to let life roll over him and Lydia didn't know how he could do it. How he could know everything that would ever happen to him and not care. How he could stick himself in one corner of the world when he hadn't even seen the rest of it.

It was embarrassing, she told him, that he had no ideas of his own.

There was a quick glimmer of fight but it didn't last. John let Lydia sum him up. He stood on the gravel, in the shade of the trees, and he looked like he believed her. Like she was right. Like he agreed that she was too good for them all.

The girls in school always wanted Lydia to tell their fortunes. They were given to accepting her authority in matters of prophecy because of her clear diction. The enunciation she learned with Ms Harvey.

Rich. Famous. Married. Dead.

The possibilities are preserved so long as the paper stays small and strong, so long as you are careful with the overlapping folds. Lydia doesn't remember the rhyme they said as they jumped through the numbers, only the power she felt when she held out their fate.

Lydia doesn't believe in fate. She chose John at Club Max in Clonmany because they had played on the same under twelve team and John used to pass her the ball. Because she used to deliver milk to his house in the mornings with Sam. Three litres of green milk on the window ledge of the gate-house. She kissed John because he was quiet but had a nice smile and cool trainers. She chose to fall in love with John and he suited her until she thought of something better. Leaving John was her choice, her mistake, and there was no fate or destiny to blame.

On the way home from choir, Dolly was all smiles. She wanted to know if Lydia had seen John. Wasn't he looking very well? Wasn't he sort of filled out, sort of grown into himself? It was lovely, Dolly said, to see him getting involved now that he was back home. Just the sort of man they needed in the town. God, Dolly couldn't get over it. John Glen in the choir and him looking so well.

A Mince Dinner

D oes Ellen definitely eat mince do you think?
    Why wouldn't she eat mince?

Lydia says nothing. She goes to the fruit bowl and presses a thumb into the avocados to see if they're ripe.

It's good steak mince, says Dolly.

Lydia is sure it's the best of good mince but she doesn't know if that will make a difference. She texts Tom and he says Ellen isn't fussy but that doesn't reassure Lydia. She looks up a recipe for vegetarian tacos with fried beans in honey, garlic and cumin. She'll make a big salad, a fresh salsa and guacamole. She has the table set in the dining room where the sage-green paint suits the delicate cornicing and the mahogany table. They'll use plain cutlery and have no flowers because Lydia doesn't want to look like they're trying.

The door is opening and Ellen comes in first. Oh my

God, she says, it smells amazing in there. What are you making?

Dolly nearly sings to see Ellen coming. Doesn't she look lovely and isn't that a beautiful coat! The bowls on the counter? She's only soaking fruit for the Christmas cakes. She's very late on the go this year. She mightn't even bother with any marzipan.

Lydia is smiling because Ellen raises smiles from everybody. So bright and energetic. So blond.

Did yous make that pavlova you were on about?

We did and it was lovely. Wasn't it, Tom?

Oh it was divine, he says from the fireplace, warming the backs of his legs. You're some ticket now, he says, domestic and everything, and he pulls Ellen in beside him, kissing her jokingly like he's madly besotted. You'll be boiling spuds next, he says. Ellen squirms away, not sure they should be kissing so publicly.

Just as they're getting ready to eat, Sam appears and they all joke about the nose on him and how he could always smell the dinner, even from the top fields. Ellen sticks up for Sam and he says it's good to finally have an ally. He has a terrible hard time of it in this house.

Ellen doesn't take any of the mince but says three times how tasty the beans are and Lydia is vindicated.

When they're finished eating but before Dolly gets up to tidy, Tom says he has a bit of news. He says he didn't want to speak until it was sorted, but he's nearly there now and he wants them to know that he's buying a bit of extra ground. The two wee fields over next to the Well Field in Carrick.

Him and Ellen are looking to build a house, he says. What did they think of that for an idea?

That's a good one, says Sam. Is that the Yelper field?

It is, aye. And Oregon's too.

That's wet ground, Tom. Rocky, says Sam.

I know. It's not that we'll put the house there. We just want the privacy of the lane. It means the farm will be unbroken over as far as the Mass Rock. Apart from the Well Field and that's only Lydia's.

Dolly thinks it's a fantastic idea. It will be great to have yous so close, she says.

That's it, aye. And we'll be neighbours, Lydia. If you ever get a move on with Bee's place.

Lydia smiles and says that would be amazing. She keeps up with the excitement, with the details of the plan, but she can't help looking at the dresser on the far wall, covered in old trophies. One or two of them belong to Tom, for football or athletics, but the majority are hers. Shields and cups and medals for singing, drama and piano. A record of winning.

And there's Tom, picking a place to live and enclosing it. Sort of nervous telling them, sweet, looking over and back at Ellen, very proud. Lydia is happy for them. It's hard not to be when they're all invited in. Like Tom and Ellen's love belongs to the whole family. Like it's something they all can share. A collective glory.

Tom knew better what to hold on to. He's the winner now, letting everyone close to the purity of what him and Ellen feel for each other. It must be something that exists.

It must be something that is possible to feel because Lydia is watching it across the table.

Late in the evening, after a few glasses raised to the future, when Tom and Ellen had left and Dolly was dozing in the top sitting room, Dan sends Lydia a picture of him eating a cream horn. She has to laugh at the nerve of him. A bit cheeky really when he hardly knows her. A messy photo with cream all over his smiling mouth.

You were right, it says. *Cream buns are what we all need.*

The Village Green

T he Sunday session in Malin Town is Dan's favourite
night of the week. Beards and hats and waistcoats,
class harmonies and one harmonica. It starts early in the
evening and that's why Cahir agrees to drive Dan. It's
the sort of place where everyone can play the guitar and
where singing might catch among the crowd. Where the
whole bar might sing a song each. It's the sort of place,
out on the edge, where they stay up until all hours with
no thought of the morning.

The door is inset with frosted glass and printed with
cursive red letters. Inside, the fire is blazing in the grate, the
dark slab floor glowing. The benches and stools are taken
and a crowd is gathered at the bar, looking back toward
the door, toward the two men in the corner seat beside the
fire, throwing it off them, a guitar and a microphone
each.

Dan sits with Oisín, Rory and Cahir, away from the fire. The girls behind the bar are cursing the fairy lights and every chancer who says he'll have a hot whiskey for the night and the cold that's in it. The kettle is going ninety to keep pace and they all want a piece of it. It's as big a crowd as could fit comfortably.

The cloves and the lemon and the sugar are helping Dan with his whiskey and the singing would hold up anywhere. A kind of rightness. A sort of simplicity in them. In the outrageous ability of the singers. In them all crowded together in a cosy room. Dan is nodding along to the beat and they all roar after every song. Two girls start dancing in the narrow path from the door to the bar.

Dan's chest is open and his shoulders down, completely relaxed since Lydia replied to him. He was all nerves until she sent him back a picture. A black and white picture of a rough wooden surface. Close up, so you could see the old grain of the wood and the outline of a star carved in it.

When Marty and Dave take their half-time break, Oisín and Rory get up to chat but Dan stays sitting with Cahir. The boys are looking to move on. Dan knows they're looking to go back to Carn, to drink in Toner's until the bus comes for Liberties. He can hear Rory telling Marty about the jumper he's wearing. How he's going to say that his granny knitted it and that she died yesterday. Try and get a sympathy shift.

Dan laughs but he stays sitting with Cahir. He feels a responsibility to Cahir in crowds. They have a long history in crowds together. From when they used to meet all the boys from Churchtown to play 40/40 and wrestling. Cahir wasn't the best at any of the games but the other boys knew that they had to hold their tongue or else Cahir and Dan would both leave and they didn't want that because Dan was the best footballer, even when he was only seven or eight. He was quick-footed. Very light and nimble. Just a natural.

Dan did try and teach Cahir a few basic skills in the back street and on the front lawn. Enough to pass himself and to get through a few lunchtimes. You don't have to be the best, he said. Just get stuck in. Cahir couldn't seem to get control of his feet. They were never where they should be. He had trouble committing to the physical shapes that are needed to master the ball, to skip past the other players. His body always let him down, and no amount of practice in the back street seemed to fix it.

Once, up at Glacks', a whole group of them went down a steep tarred brae on some toy trikes and Liam Diver threw a rock in front of Dan near the bottom of the brae. The wheel of the trike hit the rock and the trike didn't turn like it was supposed to. Dan was thrown from the seat into a fence post, his belly cut on the barbed wire. Dan was crying and the other boys didn't know what to do. Liam was saying that he was OK. Stop crying. It was his own fault.

Dan was scared by the blood and he was asking for Cahir. Looking around for Cahir's face. Where's Cahir?

Stop crying you wee gayboy. Liam pushed Cahir out toward Dan but Cahir turned back and tossed Liam to the ground and punched him in the face. He punched him until Liam was bleeding worse than Dan. Then he got up and took Dan home. Dan was afraid to tell their mum and dad so Cahir cleaned and disinfected the cut and checked on it day after day until it healed into a very thin, barely noticeable line.

Dan is trying to stop Cahir being afraid. To say that he should give the boys a chance now they're grown. They're not that bad or anything. Groups of boys are no scarier than anything else. He doesn't want Cahir cut off like the ones he sees in the shop. Hardly able to talk they're that used to quiet. Unsure. Scowling. Throwing the groceries and the money on to the counter, a plastic bag folded into a tight square in their pocket. The inside of the bag smelling like turf or sweat.

Cahir has been doing really well. Dan can tell that Rory and Oisín like him. He was smiling, nodding to the music. Happy to be out. He laughed at Rory's jokes and the girls dancing in front of the singers. He bought a round for the boys even though he's only on the sparkling water. If he stayed out long enough he would learn something about a crowd. He could stay out but he won't. He'll have some excuse to get away. He's driving. He has work. So he can get to bed at his right time. So he's away before people get drunk and try and talk to him. He'll not be able to sit for much longer with the heat roaring from the open fire. Not in those boots. Not when he didn't take off his coat.

Oreos and Stetsons

It is mayhem in the run-up to Christmas. Dan is doing five days a week since Tiernan quit. He's in charge of a full section now and he had to go to the trade show in Punchestown where they order all the sweets and the drink and the turkeys. They're starting to look at Dan for instructions, the part-timers and even the old-timers. They come up to Dan when they've finished a task and expect him to assign another. He's only a chargehand but they see that he's competent. That he's on good terms with the bosses. That John leaves the day's work with Dan to make sure it's done.

That's leadership, John told him. That's a great sign on you. He said he'd like to clone Dan. It'd be an easy life, he said, if he had a whole team like Dan.

Yesterday, they had a one-day mega-deal on Oreo gifting tins and the people of Carn were off their rockers for it.

Two-fifty was wile cheap. They hadn't enough stock for the full day never mind until Sunday. They're already nervous about next Thursday because the big slabs of beer are going half price and they're not even going to bother making a display. They're going to bring out the cages and open the doors. Let them tear away. You wouldn't have a tower built before it's dismantled anyway.

They have the Christmas tasting night coming up and everyone will get a free portion of turkey and ham. Santa will come on the fire engine, standing on the front of the truck, like he's the figurehead of a ship, with a red suit and a white beard and a big sponge belly. In his fur-trimmed sack, there'll be empty boxes wrapped in decorated paper. He'll get a Garda escort through the crowds and they'll build a gazebo for him under the tree in the car park where he'll take pictures with wains and give them treats. There'll be carol singers and a brass band and they'll play 'Feliz Navidad' because that's their signature tune. The car park tree is tall and sharp, with the lights streaming out from floodlight to floodlight. The lights are white and exact. Tiny, wavering twinkles in large enough numbers for make-believe.

It's all very festive now. Even John is wearing a Christmas jumper to work. Red with a reindeer face and a light-up Rudolph nose. Tinsel swings in thick garlands down the aisles and 'Fairytale of New York' is on the speakers every ninety minutes. All of the display units are stacked high with mince pies and fruit puddings that have oranges baked in the middle of them. Everything is sparkly and wrapped in gold packaging and most people are careful to buy a bit of that shimmering stuff when they're loading bags of coal into their car boots and bottles of Smirnoff into their handbags.

On the staff night out, they got a five-course feast and special entertainment from country music sensation Jim Callaghan in the Ballyliffin Hotel and Leisure Centre. On the bus out from Carn, Lydia was opposite Dan, in beside Katie the Mean, an actress and playwright who works the weekday cleaning shift, seven until noon. Deirdre, Elaine and Laura were sat in the back row passing cheap Cava between them, sharing the bottles around the bus, a tight bit of work getting them dispatched before Ballyliffin.

In the hotel, the lobby was pink and gold like clouds in a sunset. The shiny peach tiles looked a bit like marble, and ornate French-looking sofas crowded the room. There was a faint smell of chlorine coming up the stairs from the swimming pool. On their way into the function room, a girl in a white shirt and a black tie asked them if they wanted turkey, roast beef or salmon, and said they were at table 14. It was a long table, the full length of the dance floor, long enough to seat all forty-two of them.

Dan had to watch Lydia from six settings apart, over plates covered in gravy and half-drained glasses of stout. Some of them had already pulled their crackers and were wearing the paper crowns in their hair. They were laughing hard and Dan could see their teeth were stained with red wine and cheap coffee that tasted like cigarette smoke. The girls were all tassels and glitter, bronze tits and high set hair except Lydia whose skin was bare and white. Her neck and her shoulders were bare. Her collarbones and her arms. The top of her back and enough of her chest too. She had something in her hair that was wet-looking, that made it look thick, like she'd come from the bath and tied it back loosely without thinking in a single reach. Dan shifted in his seat with the idea of letting it down.

John bought them a few rounds of drink and there was a free mulled wine on the way in the door. By the time they had finished the trio of desserts they were balubas. They'd clean lost their senses.

At the Secret Santa, Deirdre got Fiona a pair of Christmas-tree sunglasses and a mug that said 'Live Love Sparkle'. Mickey got Steve a fart machine, and Damien, thinking the whole thing stayed anonymous because that's what they did in his old job in Derry, bought Katie a pair of edible pants and a sort of ping-pong ball for her vagina.

Jesus Christ, you sicko. What do you think we are, a crowd of pervs?

Mickey and John and Steve all went on rounds of Jameson and when Big Jim Callaghan sang 'Come Out, Ye Black and Tans', Steve was on the table, fists pumping, slurring.

When there was nobody looking straight, Dan asked Lydia to teach him how to jive. She was coming back in from the dance floor with Katie, barefoot, and Dan met them. He held his hand out and said, Come on. You'll teach me, will you?

She laughed and looked at Katie, then walked out to the floor. She took Dan's two hands and said she would have to be the man first. The man coordinates the spins, she said. Dan couldn't help smiling and Lydia smiled back at him. A curl of her small glossed lips. Their eyes were locked and Dan knew he would do whatever she said, that he would be safe in doing it because they were alone. The other couples were only pretend.

Lydia started swinging their arms and counting to Big Jim. They were going much slower than everyone else. Their hands stayed in hold and on the turns Lydia had to reach up high to let Dan stoop under her arm, grazing against her body. She kept the ritual to a simple pattern of arms and feet, spins and twirls and after a few runs through, Dan told her he had it. He knew it now. Let him be the man again.

Jim was singing with an American accent and a Stetson. The dance floor was full of shiny-backed waistcoats and shirt tails trailing over backsides housed too snug. The blue and red and yellow lights bounced over them and the amplified band and Dan couldn't believe she was in front of him, much too good for that place. Spinning together. Her laughing as Dan got into a rhythm of his own. Them never fully matching the beat of the music or the other couples. Her spinning and her dress coming a little away from her legs, the material of it clinging to her body in motion. The sequence of turns and twirls was easy and repetitive. Dan moved from one to the other and he would have kept turning through them the whole night, for the sight of her barefoot on the sprung dance floor.

She was trying to tell him something but he couldn't hear in the noise, even when she came cheek to cheek, her lips almost at his ear. She was walking away but looking back, asking why he wasn't coming. Dan followed her to the front bar, bought her a vodka and soda water and they stood in the peach foyer. Dan doesn't remember exactly what he said but he knows he was chatting shite. He does remember the feel of her reaching up and pulling him close. He remembers how little the fabric of her dress kept them apart. Just a hint of a thing between his hands and the small of her back. Them melted together in the pink and gold sunset and the thump of the heaving dance floor.

In the novelty photo booth she sat on his knee. They wore Santa hats and tinsel necklaces and for one set of photos Dan kissed her on the cheek, at the edge of her lips. The photos printed in a strip and she took them, folded them and put them in Dan's shirt pocket.

When Big Jim and the band were finished, they had to wait on their bus. A lot of the group had broken up and Steve was sleeping on the table. Dan was coming back from the pisser, telling himself no more whiskey because they were going to the nightclub and he was going to kiss her properly in the dark. When they got on the bus, he couldn't find her. Katie said she'd gone home alone.

In the shop, Dan loves the songs and the general feeling of mania. On Black Eye Friday, most people get their Christmas holidays and spend the afternoon in the pub and men are scrapping in the street by early evening. Different ones be in asking Dan about his holidays. Back in Boxing Day, he says to them and they love to hear it. There is a huge crate beside the tills for donations to the

St Vincent de Paul and it's almost full. Decency is common and called out by tradition. The 23rd December is turkey day and it's a danger to all involved. You should see them in queuing at seven in the morning to pick up their bird. Six hundred turkeys dispatched, full weight, boned and rolled, or just the crown.

How many people would 14lbs feed? Dan hadn't a notion.

It is the busiest day Dan has ever seen in the shop. A coordinated gale of resolution and activity, that's what it takes to keep the whole rolling apparatus in line, gently nudged, tugged and spun like one of the trollies with a bad wheel. Dan never stops all morning. The sheer quantity of food put through the till is crazy. He tries his might to keep the Brussels sprouts and red cabbages piled high but there is no beating them. He's flat out all day and then he stays an extra half an hour just bringing empty trollies to the trolley bay. They are queuing for trollies too. They had to pull Michael in from the forecourt to act as car park attendant.

It's a heroic bit of work. Keeping everything moving. They are heroes and they are feeling their own goodness keenly. They are there for the people who need them. They are part of the place. Dan is spinning between his jobs with a beatific understanding and love of the general goodness of Carol and Sharon and James-Anthony who are in looking to chat even on the busiest day of the year. He is overwhelmed with compassion for them, looking to be part of it. Coming so that they can feel the mayhem too, before they go back to quiet houses. Dan is sure that he loves them and wants them to know that he does. He

95

looks them deep in the eyes. Complete sincerity. He wants them to feel the connection. He wants them to know they are equal to all the others, to the ones with huge trollies filled with fancy wrappers. That at heart they are the same, so fuck your titles, and your salary scales. It's revolution to look at each other sincerely and to love each other before we die.

He thinks he'll buy Cahir a Millionaire Raffle ticket as a joke. It's only a waste of money, not resources. Dan doesn't normally play the Lotto but it is a good topic for riling Cahir.

A poor man's tax, Dan. That's what the Lotto is. It's only for desperate people with nothing left. It's all anybody would know you for.

Dan says Cahir would come round to the idea and that it would solve their practical problems. Sure their thinking time is severely curtailed with all the practical problems. With the Millionaire Raffle, somebody has to win and Cahir must admit that's different.

He might write him out a wee card saying thanks. That he knows what Cahir does for him. Lifting and laying. Driving him about. Cahir is always doing things for him. He could say that he loves lying at the TV with Cahir or sitting in the green velvet chair upstairs in the Good As New. That he knows he's the one who makes Cahir laugh. He could admit that he says things specifically so that Cahir will laugh.

Well, you have loads of options. Don't worry. You'll get there in your own time. That's what they say to Dan in the shop. Trying to keep him calm. Not understanding that

Dan's as calm as could be. That Dan wanted to stay. He might write that; if Cahir thinks it's OK, he'll stay about for another while. Like, there's no rush. Cahir would love that. Secretly. Deep down. That would be a great present for Cahir. If Dan was to stick around at home a bit longer.

I Pray for Snow

Midnight Mass is rowdier than Cahir would like. With more ordinary prayer content than he would choose. All the normal professions and not nearly enough incense. Cahir comes for the music and the sound of chanting but he is not a worshipper. He is not a participant. He doesn't bless himself, or kneel, or make the sign of the cross on his forehead, lips or heart. The rough granite pillars glint with inset shining stones and are plastered up and down the nave and transepts with coloured depictions of the wise men and the manger. Of their gifts to the baby and his mother. New gods under a cloven sky. The children had a space under their picture to inscribe a prayer, a Christmas wish, and some of them could have done with closer supervision.

The choir sits in front of the organ, a wooden giant, clambering high up the wall to the sills of the stained glass. The front bench sopranos sit under the boughs of the Jesse Tree. A thirty-foot evergreen, strung with white and silver bows.

Tracey Burns, the vet, is doing the first reading. She's a bit stagey. Clunky. But they have a hard time gathering volunteers and Tracey is thought very literate. At the end of the reading, they all give thanks, and then Lydia the Master stands up at a microphone. There is a harp set up beside the baptismal font and a lady from the Malin Road starts playing it and Lydia sings an Irish carol. Of a night in Bethlehem and shepherds on a lonely hillside. She sings cleanly, simply, and Cahir hears a tremble in her voice, a hint of fear in the words he doesn't fully understand.

When the song is over Lydia sits down and they don't clap. It wouldn't have been right. Cahir can see her face. Unsettled. Unsure. Looking ahead. Watching the strain in her gaze, at the sight of her shrinking back, it's easy to understand a fascination. Cahir was in school with Lydia and everybody fancied her then too. She was so nice and it was easy for her to be nice, talking to Cahir in the break of their Chemistry double period. Asking him did he want anything back from the vending machine. Asking him to explain the covalent bonding structures of carbon compounds. She said Cahir explained it better than Mr McGuinness, how some of the atoms were so reactive that they would bond to almost anything, so unstable by themselves that they had to get fixed to another element. She liked that idea, she said. She needed a story to go with all the little drawings.

Cahir never saw her look as well as just now. She'd given

up on distance and taken the risk of asking them to listen, not sure if it was worth it, ecstatic vulnerability flowing out of her. It was the first time Cahir saw the full beauty of her, white and smooth like an idol to lie before.

Father McDaid is reading a list of baby names. The name of every baby christened in the parish this year. Seventy-eight names. And there is to be a Christening tonight, he announces. A shuffle is heard in the pews. A new little Jesus is very nice for the family of the infant saviour, less nice for the rest of them struggling past bedtimes. Them with dolls' houses to assemble and trampolines to erect, bicycles and trikes to set out. Sacks to be filled, biscuits and carrots nibbled, notes tucked behind candlesticks so that wish lists come true.

The lucky family march up to the altar and take their positions. Father McDaid is there with the microphone and a little table for all his props. It looks like they're having a bit of bother with the young godfather. The baby's dad is having a word in his ear and looks to be holding the back of his jacket. Holding him up straight. Father McDaid has a few questions for them.

Do they reject the glamour of evil and refuse to be mastered by sin?

They do.

Surely. That's the stuff. It's better to be certain. Ironclad. Assent granted to every tenet, on the record, slipped into the gaps of Father McDaid's swinging inflection. Blessed be the obliging godparents. They are ours now. But maybe the wee babby will settle and they'd all say anything for the babby to settle. It is absolutely screaming the place down.

Do they reject Satan, Father of Sin and Prince of Darkness?

That's an easy one. The would-be-godfather leans close to the mic, in over the top of the new daddy, the sound of him wetting his lips clear over the speakers.

Aye, he says, and fuck the devil too.

His denunciation is stifled after that, laughter pulling away from the microphone, echoing into the high dome above him, the new daddy coming between the boy and amplification. Fixed smiles all around and a burly relative from the front row is quick to the altar steps, clamping an arm around the boy's waist and bundling him toward the side door. There is a call from the pews, a holler and a clap, and two other young men follow them out.

The crowd is in shock. Mortified for the poor family. Not sure if they should laugh or feign deafness. In fairness to Father McDaid, he recovers brave and quick. An old pro, he doesn't let the crowd get restless.

That's a new one, he says to polite laughter. After that it's a whole race. They can hardly make out the words of his other questions, he goes that fast, throwing them handily from the tip of his tongue. The baby is anointed and wet from the silver jug but he cries on, screams on. And the parents with thunderous faces, in adherence to the pre-arranged staging of the event, sit on the altar, either side of a crib, holding hands as the baby lies between them wailing. The picture of goodness at the break of Christmas Day.

Before the end, under the circular chandelier, the horos and the dome, Father McDaid is lit beautifully. He gestures wide at the surrounding splendour, the flower spikes and shining gold, the crisp vestments and polished pews, and in front of the biggest audience of the year all are especially thanked. Vera and the choir. The Legion of Mary. The Pioneers. Talented local electrician Jackie Gallagher who puts on a lighting display you wouldn't see this side of Antrim Cathedral. Did you know there are more altar servers in Carn Chapel than in the whole city of Derry? There is a round of applause for Michaela Canny who washes and irons their costumes and for the men who count the money on a Monday. The Bethany Bereavement Group get a run out along with the Accord Marriage Counsellors, the golf classic committee, and finally, the Good As New.

As you all know, Father McDaid says, we said goodbye to a great servant this year, Mary Margaret McLaughlin the Painter. (Applause.) I want to pay a very special tribute to Mary Margaret and to all who have helped continue her good work. Especially that is, to young, em, to, ah, young . . .

Father McDaid doesn't know Cahir. They have met a few times but he doesn't know Cahir's name. He's searching his page but the pause is too obvious and too long. He looks underneath the lectern but there are no answers to be found. Better to move on and get this show finished. He looks back at them, arms wide and simpering.

A very special thank you to you *all*, he says.

There is an attempt then to go in peace but Cahir doesn't move. He waits in his pew until the crowds are gone, until the money baskets are tidied away and the altar is cleared, until the organist closes and locks the lid. As the overhead spots are darkened, the alcove behind the Jesse Tree glows with candlelight. Cahir moves toward the candles and the heat of the little flames rises into his face, the air wavering between him and the ambry. A gold box set into the wall, stocked with pure olive oil in ornately stoppered glass bottles. The chrism scented with balsam. Simmered over fires that are fed with old, disfigured icons and sweet smelling extracts. Every batch of oil mixed with some drops of older oil, an unbroken chain back to the Apostles.

Cahir is not upset at the slight. He couldn't care less about parish fundraising or having his name read from the stage. In an unbroken line of ecclesiastical succession, in this place named for the rock of a church, this place of study and secret prayer, Cahir knows what's holy and what isn't. He lights two new candles from the fire of one that's near out. The earth tilts into the light.

Christmas in Effish

It's a nervous hour in Churchtown when they open the presents. They each have a spot on the different chairs where they lay out cloth sacks filled with socks, soaps and pyjamas. Cloth sacks, almost worn through. The light in the room comes from the tree and from a lamp on the piano and the fire Sam builds as soon as he's down the stairs.

Brilliant! I was telling you mine burst!

So soft. I love these.

They are careful with each other and the efforts they make. So they say what they should before there is time to love something. Then there is no clash, just a gentle frenzy and a stack of torn paper and an early breakfast of grilled bacon and cherry tomatoes, fried eggs and potato bread. A splash of Prosecco in the orange juice.

Will we roast them or boil? They were a bit sizzled last year I thought.

No, it's full weight, says Dolly. You need the bones for flavour. Take me out three decent-sized pots anyway.

When they've the pots arranged they make their rounds, reusing the gift bags from under the tree. Bringing whiskey and wine and Dolly's cakes and puddings to the aunts and uncles and Wee Susie, their neighbour on the left. It's a blessing to have a neighbour on only one side.

In Effish they hardly get a hug broken before there's chat of a whiskey or a beer.

And is this wee Jane? Dolly asks. Was Santa good? Oh my God you're a very big girl. No, thank you, darling. If I have another Quality Street I'll pop.

A hexagonal tin bright with relief passes over her and Lydia wants to trace her finger over the snow-covered roofs and the scarves of the running children. In the trail of the tin, purple and gold wrappers rustle as they're twisted off and scrunched in eager hands. It keeps passing in the seated circle they've taken up, until it returns to the corner cupboard with the golden knob. A white Stanley stove burns turf and her uncle Charlie sits beside it, and asks her will she take nothing? It's a bad house, he says, when there's nothing to offer her. Lydia says she's fine, really, but thanks very much.

They make the most of the day in Effish, God's Own Country. A day of splendour and mirth and good cheer even when you're staying off the whiskey. Tom and Sam are quickly tipsy. Charlie pours a tight measure. Water is no help to them but he sets it down in a wee jug beside them anyway. They'll not be fit to swallow a sprout much less cook one.

Dan has been wishing Lydia Happy Christmas in an old Iron Man T-shirt stretched over his shoulders, tinsel wrapped around his forehead. With their mum and dad in Peru, Dan and Cahir were to go to their aunt in Kilcar, he said, but they were staying home instead because Cahir had refused to go. He made Dan ring up their Aunt Caroline to plead illness. Cahir bought Dan an IOU for five trips to the cinema and the promise that Dan could pick the films. Apparently this was a major concession and proof of tender love because it would mean driving to Derry and listening to popcorn munchers shout over cityscape explosions. Dan bought Cahir a previously owned raincoat and a bamboo toothbrush.

Lydia sends Dan pictures of stupid things that mean nothing. Just things that look pretty or odd. It's a developing rhythm in their correspondence. He sends her back a picture with his face in it. It's funny that he thinks so much of his own face but he's right too because his face is what Lydia wants to see. She looks forward to seeing his face. Then if she doesn't reply, he'll send a text explaining what he likes about the image, what he felt when he saw it, or about the book he read in response to her writing beauty off as boring and retinal. Asking her about flowers and about furniture makers and about books.

They are getting ready now for a nut roast and in the video Dan sent Lydia was happy to see Cahir slicing carrots in his Christmas jumper, and the room strung with blue and red lights. There is a money tree near his chopping board on the kitchen island, hung with baubles. Dan says it's as far as Cahir would go because he wouldn't fell a tree and he wouldn't use the plastic one in the attic. He said it corresponds to no real species of conifer and would probably end up in the Pacific garbage patch. He'll have no part in that, he said. Lydia looks closely at Cahir, and he's not at all the boy she remembers from school. In the video Dan sent, he looks happy and relaxed. He looks like he's on the verge of dancing.

Lydia left the staff party early. She had to get away from Dan before she did something silly. She had to pull back because his eyes were so free. Scary sure. Like a memory of herself before she crawled home from Belfast. Like freedom, expansion, life opening out and not narrowing. Not a choice made, not a hope dashed. He was daring her, his hair slicked back, two heavy locks fallen over his forehead. He didn't make a declaration but he did come close in the hotel lobby, his dark-green suit stark against the peach floor tiles and the frescoed walls.

He knows he is a total saddo, he said, but he just can't get over this place. Not yet. He can't just run off like that's the only option. Number one, he said, what about the light? And the sea, he said, the fucking sea is everywhere. That isn't it though. It's more than that. And he was very sorry to be telling her sad facts about himself. But Cahir. That's his brother. She knows Cahir, right? Yeah, well, Cahir needs him.

Lydia said she was very comfortable with sad facts and she shivered at the film that came into his eye but she couldn't bring herself to the rare chance for someone to know her better. She told him nothing, just hugged him tight, shivering right out from her middle at the feel of his chest.

Dolly is now ensconced in the soft armchair with a tumbler as big as Sam's. They'll never get the turkey cooked.

Oh I can't deal with that witch of a sacristan, Dolly says. I was in Farren's with them all during the week for the Christmas do. I was ready to do her damage. Sitting in beside Father McDaid, like she was his shadow! He danced like a good one, too.

Any mention of how he's going to balance the books now that the Good As New is away downhill?

Sure is it any wonder? That wee boy from Molly's Brae, everybody is feared to go in to him. He's that odd.

They would need to publish the accounts, I don't care what anyone says.

Uncle Charlie has a way of agreeing that is only a sharp intake of breath. Committing to the record slowly, measuredly.

Were yous out this morning?

We went last night, Dolly says, and Lydia sang. Oh, and Annarita Roe said to tell you the singing was lovely, Lydia. She had tears in her eyes she said.

Annarita Roe, says Charlie, is she anything to Claire and John-Eddie?

A niece maybe, says Sam.

Lydia wasn't sure at all. She couldn't hear the harp and she started with a kind of automation, with barely a thought for the tune and rhythm she had kept in her head all day while pretending to do other things, legs relaxed, head even, chest open. The note she kept coming to from every angle, from every thought, testing herself, testing its resiliency, the hope of picking it from her register.

It was hard to know how it sounded down the aisles, how it boomed in the stone box. Afterwards, she was less relieved than she expected. Less kindly disposed than before when she was nervous. She felt separate from herself. Floaty and cut-off, fucking pissed by the time she was watching Aoife Harkin baptise a screaming baby. Aoife is a pretty girl even spread in incubation. *Jesus, Aoife Harkin is some ride*, that's what the boys used to say. Aoife could have had anyone and look at her now.

Lydia was wrecked coming off the altar after 'O Holy Night'. A little bitchy and self-pitying, picking her way carefully, watching her step on the thick, pink carpet. It was John who took a light hold of her elbow and whispered in her ear.

That was some bit of singing, he said.

Lydia's skin tightened at his hold. Remembering the other ways he used to touch her. The two of them in John's car after Liberties, idling in the yard outside her house, kissing under the orange lamps that run down to the byres. His hands frantic at her body.

How they would swim in the Foyle and the Swilly and the proper sea, and how their skin would be soft afterwards. How, once, after coming from the water at Kinnagoe, they had stood in John's very neat bedroom. The dark navy covers on his bed well smoothed. Deodorant cans on the mantel of the bricked-up fireplace. They played British indie bands on the speakers and gently, carefully undressed, their clothes dropping on to wide, sanded floorboards. Under the covers, John was on top of her, inside her, moving slowly, rocking, funny and then sore. John rigid when he heard her gasp and her having to draw her hands down his back, to motion at his hips for him to start again. She thought it was a fine attempt at sex overall and that John was good at kissing. Like he saved up all his feelings for it.

On the altar, John let go of her elbow with a smile. He had barely touched her at all.

With the widely reported success of the song, Lydia thinks maybe it was OK and forgivable to beg them for approval. She's unable to disown the reviews, unable to turn away from kind words, though she knows it's a pity to need them. Lydia is laughing. Her good form is cheap and immediate. She sits back and listens about the priests, the stations, the stipends. About who always had a face on them. Who was and who wasn't of our religion.

There was life about the town then!

It'll not go back to that!

About Pat the Darkie and Jock the Pastry Cook. About Crooked Shot, the butcher with the meat all hanging out in the shop. And they never so much as *heard* of food poisoning.

Dead before they could tell anyone, says Tom, leaning in over Lydia's shoulder, laughing before he gets his joke told.

The dinners they ate in that house, says Charlie. The pork chops were green. Diesel in the soup. And three or four dogs under the table scrambling for scraps. The things that lived in that woman's flour bag, he says, you wouldn't want to be sure.

Lydia only gets them home because the Effish turkey is cooked and they don't want to let it spoil and dry out. Nine pounds of dry white meat. Tom can hardly bite his finger and the other two aren't far behind. Tom lies down on the sofa and Sam sits in his chair pretending to read the back cover of a novel he was given, dozing inside thirty seconds. Dolly puts up a better show. She fires the hobs and boils the kettle and unsheathes the meat thermometer. The extractor fan is humming. They get the turkey in and the vegetables on and they set the table. There is a dark holly wreath in the centre and a big white candle burning in the middle. They are ready for it by the time it's out, a fine spread. A golden turkey and a glazed ham. Herbed butter on the vegetables. Sausage stuffing and a rich gravy, goose fat roasties and two silver dishes of cranberry sauce.

We're away to the dogs this year, Tom says. No crackers at all to pull?

Or napkins, Dolly says.

I'm joking, Mum! Sit down. It's gorgeous.

Well, you may thank Lydia for saving the day. We'd be lying in a ditch at the foot of the hill if it wasn't for her. Tom raises his glass.

A toast, he says. To our wee Christmas saviour!

After the late dinner they're not fit for much. Tom is away to Malin for a Christmas sing-song and Lydia sits in the top room for a short while before climbing the creaking stairs, dazed from the glow of the fire and the wine she had after her pudding.

New Year's

L ydia gets out of her bed glad to see the end of the night. She couldn't settle. She was aware of herself overheating, tossing. At the sink, there is a plate of bones and chicken skin and other scraps, and the smell is rich and sick. She should throw it out to the cats in the yard but she hates how they come running at her feet, tripping her before she can get to the base of the alder tree. None of them are pets exactly. None of them are wild completely. Most nights a scrappy nameless tomcat is at the back door or under the windowsill and they throw him gristle and sausages that are going hard. He has big scabby eyes and hairless patches and is sometimes good and fat but mostly war-torn lean. Her dad calls him pussycat and pretends he's a girl but maybe wild cats are always girls, like tractors. Lydia brings the plate outside in her bare feet, the ground screaming up her legs and into the backs of her knees. The pain screaming through her nerves is like breakfast.

Dolly says all the choir ones are invited to the party, even John Glen.

There are no flowers to pick, just more holly. They have sprigs of holly everywhere. Lydia and Dolly spend the day arranging holly sprigs and chopping salad components. The fires are all lit and died down, simmering bombs made of milk cartons and slack coal. The stars are out since half-five, the piano is shining in the lamplight. The table is full, even lengthened with its middle insert; cold meats and olives, pickles and salads, silver platters and bowls of rosy glass. Careful displays with oversized spoons for the gradual diminishing as the crowds file past with their gold-rimmed plates, picking Parma ham and smoked salmon and a spoon of home-made tartar sauce. A squeeze of lemon and a drizzle of vinaigrette and a big wedge of Dolly's wheaten bread. The table wouldn't hold them eating at once so they stand at counters or sit with their plates balanced on their knees, judging the right place to pierce a cherry tomato, that won't send it bouncing across the Ulster carpet.

Would you ever get Kitty a drink?

The crystal is shining in the back kitchen and the cupboard above the air fryer is full to the back with wine bottles. Lydia opens a French red without a notion if it's a good one. She pours herself a glass and takes a big sup. It's very floral.

With a gulp, Lydia remembers the trifle.

She puts down her glass and carries it to the cake table,

making space for the cut-glass bowlful of Dolly's illicit slash-mara: tinned fruit, thickset custard and home-made sponge soaked in poitín. When Dolly was a girl the stills were hid in the slunks over Effish, where the guards were feared to lose their footing and drown in one of the marshy sinkholes. Now, they get the poitín distilled from a steel vat in Clonmany and Dolly's trifle has the ICA seal of approval, shiny and wobbling, spooned into china bowls with loosely whipped cream.

In the early evening it's only the relations who hope to get home early. The McQuillans are first. Harold and Rosemarie, solicitor husband and wife with a practice in Buncrana. First cousins of Lydia's dad. They've brought their wee grandson Harry. A dote going round the knees, not a bit strange. Dolly has him on her lap, bouncing staccato. She has no fear of him and that seems to keep his whinge away. Harry's frown flattens every time she starts up again, instantly forgetting, roaming with no intent.

My aunt Jane, she brought me in,
she made me tea in a wee black tin

I swear that child was never fully tamed, his granny says.

Oh no. That's not right. You're not a gurney gister. Don't listen to granny. You're a wee dote. That's what you are. A pure dote.

Dote? Harry repeats the last word back to them, trying to copy Dolly but with such big eyes.

The Glacks come in and the furore starts again. A drink? Grab a plate! That's wee Harry from Buncrana. Isn't he a dote? Isn't it freezing? And where is Tom, leaving Lydia to this? Ailish Glack comes over and gives Lydia a big hug. Hello! We missed you on Christmas Day, she says. Oh my God that dress is fab!

Thanks! I know, they're wile men. We barely got the dinner made.

Serious? Oh my God. Well? How are you? Are you still doing the art?

The horrible perfumed depth of that wine would suit Lydia now. For diving in. For drowning happily. Splish splash splosh, laughing as she sinks. Bye bye! All the laughing masks are drowning but none as happy as her! Ailish is wearing too much make-up.

Still about here, Lydia says. Working away. Are you still in Dublin?

Yeah. I can't see myself coming back anytime soon to be honest. I've my own team now and it's just *very* busy. Never say never, you know.

That is *great*! Let me get you a drink though. Mum would kill me if she saw my shite hosting skills. What are you having?

I'll just have a whiskey please. No ice.

No bother, Lydia says smiling, scolding herself all the way to the kitchen. Stop it. Stop it. Ailish is just trying to be nice. Have a look at yourself, please. She's hardly any better. Trying to impress everyone with her hosting. Hairless from the eyelashes down. Skirt up to her arse.

They are finishing the food and the empty bottles are

piling at the side of the scullery sink. There will be a call to sing something and Lydia is trying to list the songs she knows, lyrics and tune. She is all dread and desire at the thought. Like every time she ever does it. Like the first time she did, as a grown woman, sing to them in a quiet room for their entertainment. It's worse and worse the more you love something, the more you long to be good, and it's no cure no matter how well it goes, no scores are erased in glory. Lydia doesn't cope well with glory anyway. Better to have it over. Thanks very much. I'm sure it was grand, yeah. You're very kind. It's a nice song, isn't it?

She unsettles herself and for what? For any meagre fulfilment she can catch and roll out from the lumps she inherited. She'll do the best she can. The McCarrons are in from Cabbeydooey and there is great music in that family as Dolly never tires of saying. Mrs McGinley is there with the Roe sisters. They'll have their songs ready. They probably have sheet music with them. Anthony and Jeffery will sing too. Old hands, they'll not even try and decline. There's no sign of John. Lydia didn't think he would come. There was a small chance, maybe, after he heard her sing at Mass. She was ready just in case, but he won't come now so close to midnight.

Tom and Ellen are in the lower sitting room. Lydia pulls her skirt down her thighs and tries to catch Tom for a smile about Dolly but Tom is looking at Ellen. It would be nice to have somewhere to look for the countdown. All of the couples are pairing off. The tyranny of New Year. Still, it's a charming set up with Dolly as queen of the country and them around her.

Not long now!

I know, can you imagine? They don't be long flying in.

That was one quick year, I'll tell you.

To the one that's coming, Sam says, and the health to enjoy it.

They clink glasses and sip. Sam is done up in clean heavy cloth, the only kind that's natural to him and he drinks Bushmills from the one tumbler. Lydia tries to stay beside him. To stay relaxed. It's a battle she loses because at half-eleven, Tom and Ellen come in from the rose beds engaged to be married and Lydia puts down her tray of crab and salmon toast.

The party roars with joy. Dolly and Sam are only letting the lovebirds go as the news filters out. Lydia is over and has them hugged straight away. The walls are coming at them with big smiles wishing them all the happiness in the world and sure they'll have it because the two of them are made for each other. Who could ever deny it? Lydia can hardly speak. She is buoyed up with more joy than she has ever felt before. Better by far than any happiness of her own. She only hopes they love each other in the way she imagines. She hopes the stories that carry them are lasting, a fixed trove that will span every barren stretch. If such a thing is possible then they deserve it. To think of a house with Tom and Ellen in it, children brought up noisily, it's enough hope for any night. Even New Year's night. Ellen is glowing, glimmering, shining in the middle of her new family. They forget to do a proper countdown and nobody cares and they open champagne and sing on for the night. Dolly sings three times. Sam plays the piano and when Lydia sings 'Auld

Lang Syne', she means her good wishes down into her bones. They dance and jump, swinging and jiving, hugging, crying, smiling until four in the morning and the betrothed are long slipped away.

Stocktake

Cahir writes it all down. So there's no forgetting. The creams and fats, the sweets, the starches, all the different names for sugar. He keeps a pile of the empty pots and cartons and wrappers until he can do the math. The values and limits exceeded in hunger, lust and binge. The violent rush of the food. The horrible surge of it in his blood. Too much to use. It was the equivalent of three or four days eating and the days must be repaid. That's how you restore balance. That's the cycle: feast then fast. A corporeal penance. Dirty, then clean.

Graham and Marie have been ringing them flat out. Nervous that they're abandoning their only children at a sensitive time of the year. Cahir actually likes the look of them on the camera, thrown into distortion. With their features the wrong way round, it's a little easier to stomach them, talking about panettone and how the boat people of

Lake Titicaca make everything out of rushes. How they didn't like the city of Puno at all, very cold with too many dogs, but that Cusco was lovely. How they set off on the Inca Trail on Boxing Day, got a few snaps at the Sun Gate and were back to Cusco in time for New Year's. There was a big party in the square apparently where they all dressed in yellow and ran around in circles. Marie had been worried she wouldn't be fit for Dead Woman's Pass because she struggled wile with the altitude sickness, she said.

When we came from the coast at Máncora, this lovely man taught me how to surf, and then we were straight back up the mountains. Where was that Graham? Huaraz. That's right Huaraz. I was absolutely dosed with it.

You were great honey. Heroic. After the Lost City, I knew you'd be fine. How are you both anyway? Are you looking after each other?

That was as much as Cahir could listen to. He faked a poor connection and hung up.

New Year is a hateful time. Dan is working. Stocktaking after the Christmas rush. They have to count every item in the building. Every plastic fork and knife, every packet of crisps. Anything that could be considered an asset. They go around with handheld scanners, beeping the barcodes and counting. Counting, counting, counting. Hunched, squatting, lying flat on the floor, whatever shape is best to reach the back of the shelf. Sometimes they have to take the products out, count them and then put them back in again. The shop is a right mess after.

They were doing a stocktake the day Mary Margaret's heart gave out. Cahir remembers because he ran downstairs

124

to try and find help. Dan was on the ground at the Viscount mint biscuits, reaching in the back of the shelf, concentrating. Cahir came walking down the biscuit aisle very quickly and leant to whisper in Dan's ear.

Mary Margaret's dead, he said.

Cahir had to explain to Dan, Mr Glen, Father McDaid and the guards what happened to Mary Margaret. How he had been in the back room, looking for a ledger. How Mary Margaret was so disorganised and how Cahir had told her often enough that he would organise the files for her. That she'd find it much easier if he did. That she'd called Cahir to retrieve a pair of trousers from the top shelf and how he was thinking would she not just get the stepladder? Or better yet, not pile the trousers into unsteady, wile-looking towers. Then he heard a bit of a clatter and the thud of the trousers coming down from the shelf and when he got out to her, she was lying completely still. He gave her a shake and tried talking to her and then he took her soft blue-veined wrist. He put two fingers on her pulse and there was nothing. That's all he did before he ran downstairs. He didn't even move the trousers.

When he started helping Mary Margaret on a Monday, Wednesday and Saturday, it looked like a first step and his mum and dad were delighted with it. The discharged convalescent. Maybe the great withdrawal was over because here he was, out of the house and speaking aloud to other people.

It was all very promising and healthy and they were kind about it. Cahir could see their excitement surge and gradually wane. He didn't know why he wasn't fixed. He was sorry if it wasn't enough or if he was going too slow. He wanted to say that it wasn't their fault. They didn't do anything but be kind and nice to him. He didn't know what was wrong with him. Why he couldn't look them in the eyes. Why he hated them to say his name.

A Trip to Lidl

Y ou're wearing a hat after all that?

My hair is crap, says Dan. Come on. Let's go.

It's worse than launching the *Queen Mary*, getting Dan out of the house. Even when it's him who wants to go and when he's had all morning to get ready. He was in and out of the kitchen a few different times in various states of dress and eventually, with Cahir fit to scream, almost livid, here he is in a suede bomber jacket and a plain baseball cap, hair all tucked away.

The Starlet sparks no bother and Cahir screws down his window because the rain has stopped and there is a smell of damp. The air beats their ears like they're sailing, a beat every time they pass a pole, the poles a little uneven and slung together like children on a walk to see the river or the sea, their arms linked long, their heads pitched to the sky. The plastic debris covers the floor in the back. If you worried your feet down through it, it'd come high up your calf. The rustle of it helps soothe Cahir as he propels himself, shot along with the force of internal combustion, with fumes pouring from the exhaust and with pistons pumping at the crackle of tiny fires. He tries to be economical. Get up to fifth gear and take her handy. By the time they get up to the Mintiaghs, they're sailing along and the sun is out. Cahir says Dan can play his music on the way back. Nothing shit though.

Did you see John's new car? He's the first man in Donegal with the model 3. John says the acceleration is phenomenal.

That's classic, says Cahir. Jesus, that is classic. You're not impressed by that? That's all handed to him. None of that's earned you know?

It must be better than nothing, says Dan. Sure he could have bought a Range Rover or something.

Cahir hates that Dan talks about him. As if John's doing anything worthwhile, guffawing about in exactly the most lucrative surrender. Plodding in his Clarks like an off-duty potter. Going on as if a Tesla makes up for delivering global convenience to Carn. Or for the oil swishing about in 50,000-litre tanks under the car park. Poisonous slosh and ullage. John hasn't a clue and yet it's Cahir's fate to watch him succeed at everything he tries. Even with Dan. From their desks, Cahir and John have the same view of the Malin Road and if they could wriggle out the little windows, they'd have access to the same ledge above the car park. Cahir would give John a push if he's tempted, only you shouldn't do it to the wains in Spraoi agus Spórt. Sirens and mayhem as the guards and the Fire Brigade rouse to the crisis, the two stations within sight of the ledge.

They were all home for Christmas. All the ones he used to know. Cahir tries not to see any of them, the sub-assistant, vice-regional presidents of the world. Newly promoted from among the economic migrants of Raheny. Sniffing around each other. Begging in plain pursuit. Fever and tongues out and then panting and pathetic and shrivelled, but at least finished with the goo.

Lidl are all sold out of secateurs. He should have come on Thursday the girl says. They won't be getting them in again. Not this year anyway.

That's a fucking disgrace. Jesus, that's a fucking joke. Do they think I was just looking for a run to Buncrana?

I'd say they don't give a shit, Cahir. What did you want them for anyway?

Nothing. It doesn't matter, he says. I was going to prune that thing of Mum's. That hydrangea. What will we do now?

I dunno. Let's stay out though.

And do what?

I don't know. Something fun.

Can you not just tell me what you want and stop being so annoying?

Did you see this? Dan says, handing Cahir his phone.

I don't get it.

Well, Dan says, you need to know that bit of *The Simpsons*.

They start driving, heading for Dunree, the long way back via Leenan and Dunaff. The view of the sea through Mamore is wide and high and above them the hills are dark. Smokey, like they were burnt on the barbecue. The hills ripple in the light like a well-muscled back and the broad strand of the fjord flows into the sea's great sweep.

The Swilly is deep. Full of shadow and depth, letting the light make cuts that blind you to smaller scars. That blank space is enough to calm Cahir at the edge that's hard to reach, near the cliffs where it would be technically difficult and expensive to drop concrete foundations. The rounded boundaries take every curl and slap thrown at them, letting it all run back white, streaming to gather again. They are facing the sea and everything is better. Cahir suggests they go to the fort at Leenan. OK?

Dan looks up from his phone and says, Yeah. Sounds good.

Cahir asks him what he's muttering about and Dan says he's gonna do it. He's gonna dye his hair blond next summer.

I'm glad you have such a clear plan in life, says Cahir. It's a big relief to me.

Sometimes, Cahir would love to tell Dan to wise up. Cop on. To explain about the cruelty in the world but he can't do it at Leenan, a ledge in the air with water crashing under them for miles. He pulls back from cruelty because Dan is lit from inside. Cahir feels the light on him. He gets a physical response to the frequency of the waves. A balm that's nearly always on and he gets used to it. He misses it when it's not there, he hates anything that can make it flicker or dim. Most of all he fears anything that might snuff it out. He doesn't want to ever tell Dan about the light in case thinking about it is bad for him. In case unconsciousness is essential to whatever enthusiasm or openness sustains it. In case knowing about the light becomes a burden for him.

That he would watch it too closely, smother it, mourn it and chase it. Try and recreate it using the same cheap and coarse ways that other people use when they want to be seen. Damaging ways, using themselves up as fuel, lit matches set to petrol. Immolation.

Cahir is trying to be calm and let the sea air scour him, practising an amicable face for the next set of squalid walls. He doesn't know what will happen to the light. He doesn't know if it has a natural end or lifespan. If at some point Dan will stop shining and become like everyone else. If it's uncontainable, growing too bright for one small place.

Down the lough, toward Buncrana and Rathmullen, the water is sheltered and deep and the top has settled down like glass, as if the day had got cold and sunk, puddled in sublimation. At the fort, on the edge of the open sea, the volume of clear sky would let a scream fly unheard and to the west, the hills are peaking, competing as shadows with Errigal and Muckish. Before them the collision of white as the water draws in, luminous again. Too big to capture in a photo or memory, the cliffs and the drop are the only way Cahir's ever found to get so high. Dan roams among the red-brick chimney stacks. Monuments on the abandoned shelf like a scaffold that the builders forgot. Five red chimney stacks standing in a line, rising from the rubble of the old fort at their feet. There are no proper paths. No safe areas. As you pick your way around the rocks you have to mind your feet. There are underground bunkers and passageways but Cahir doesn't let Dan go down. They are not structurally sound. Dan is taking pictures of little flowers growing on the cliff face and of the view toward Dunaff Head and Malin.

In the car, Dan lies his head back, closing his eyes. His face getting younger as creases dissipate. Cahir feels a terrible longing in his chest. He doesn't want to go home or for their trip to end. He turns on the heat and waits for the condensation to clear.

A Sudden Stratospheric Warming

The dam held. The stupid cows mustered no more threat, they just stood on the other side of his barrier, looking at him. Gurning at him. Braying at him all plaintive. As if he could feel sorry for them. As if he could imagine they needed the grazing space. Them and their fat backsides.

Cahir was glad when he saw the winter. When he saw the grass under the hedges pause, matted and limp like his hair when he should have washed it yesterday. All turgidity gone, the riot over. The cows were taken in and he had a rest in his watch. Cahir could relax once they were in the byres. They'd have been gone much earlier if the world wasn't falling apart. They'd had the longest growing season in living memory and there would be no problem with fodder this year.

But there are always other problems.

A wobbling of the Jet Stream, then collapse, compression

and reversal. An easterly continental airflow meets a storm system from the Atlantic and snow showers cover the country. We're ground to a stop and records are fallen. Six foot icicles are reported on Sliabh Sneacht and the snow-drifts are as high as windowsills. Met Éireann has issued a red weather warning and the government has told them not to leave their homes on account of drifting blizzard conditions. There isn't a loaf of bread to be had in the town. If Cahir could find some, he might start eating bread again. Now that he's so slim.

It was a strange place to eat. An unplanned meal on the drive back from Buncrana. The darkest dining room in Ireland, out the back of the hotel, like the set of a low-budget play with false sash windows and chairs painted to look heavy. There wasn't a being there and Dan wondered if they could play a game of hide-and-seek while they waited for the food. The batter on Dan's fish was soggy and Cahir thought he could plaster walls with his falafel.

It can't be possible to shit out your own fat but then, where does it go after it's flown from your connective tissue? By yesterday morning, on the glass scales in the bathroom, he was four pounds lighter. Last night he could barely scrounge a palmful of fat at each tit. This morning, hung forward, twisted every way, overhead lights lit to make humps plain, Cahir passed for lean. Lean Cahir. The sight was extraordinary. A body he hardly knows. A destiny fulfilled. The work of his slow renovation revealed to be striking and well judged. A vision of manhood is rescued from his body. He tried on all his clothes to be sure, he has been fooled before by cold hardened nipples, but they all fit him, even the polka-dot shirt. There was space in it. If he had known a bout of the shits was the answer he would have induced them years ago. He will never be fat again.

It's a cheery development. Heartening to judge himself squarely in the middle of the heap. After all the press-ups and lunges, the three-day diets of boiled eggs and cottage cheese, the seven-minute exercise videos; it was a spoiled falafel that did the job. He should contact the hotel. Tell them they have a revolution on their hands. Put them in fancy wrappers. Say they're like protein balls, except they make you puke your insides up.

When you have the right shape, you can chance a bit of friction. A bit of touching. Touching other bodies. If he thought he was thin enough, Cahir might join the gym. Maybe he'll buy a sports T-shirt, something with a logo, now that he is going to be flat-chested.

The temperatures haven't risen above freezing in several days. The gritters are tramping the roads morning and evening, spewing rock salt on the main routes. Driven into the road, ground down, to lower set points in a new coat of brine. To grip wayward tyres. The back roads and hillsides are treacherous with black ice. School buses stay on the main roads and if you live on a steep enough hill, you'll get a few days off school. Cahir and Dan never got any days off because they could walk from Molly's Brae. The footpath between the Cross and the school was the only likely place for a fall.

Cahir is nervous about the weather. It's an external condition he can't temper or control and the potential extremes of it are frightening. That some combination of forces might conspire to deny him his chance at legacy, his apology for a wrecking life.

When the forecasts came in first, Cahir was glad of the opportunity for activity. There isn't much caring to be done in winter. No competitors to cut back, nothing fresh or juicy for a roaming predator to graze. Most days Cahir just walks through the old woods, coming to his slope from different angles and picturing it growing up to screen the lane and the distant rooftops.

With extreme threats getting broadcast on the radio, Cahir went to the Co-op and bought a big roll of muslin netting and cut it into squares. He draped it over the trees, semi-sheer fleece hoods fastened with twine at the base, like body bags stood up on the crunchy muck, like young scarecrows on a battlefield.

They say survival should be no problem. That they are adaptable things with received ideas about staying alive. Cahir is afraid they might not have learned correctly. That the band of displaced loners, out here in ground they don't know, might not have planned correctly. That they wouldn't have enough sugar stored, packed under the bark and in the roots. That they would have been too happy, not afraid at all, that they would have had water coursing through them when the hard frosts came, that the sapwood was too wet and that little veins might have frozen and bust.

They should know what they're doing, it's their inheritance to know, but Cahir can't trust that. Not when they're so small. Not when the air is turned abnormal. How can anyone tell him what will happen in a world no one understands? Doling out advice based on past performance. On how things grew during the lucky human blip.

Before the snow, in a mist that was too heavy to rise, too thick and sweet with turf smoke to lift, Cahir came back to take the muslin off, exposing their slight bodies from under their new coats. So the snow wouldn't gather and crush them. To let snow fall to the ground through a diverging leaf-bare structure. To make it hard for snow or rain to weigh down their spindly dendritic arms.

Cahir changes his shoes for wellington boots. He pulls them out of a green rucksack that Dan got free at soccer camp. His step across the field is a powdery crunch. He shakes the snow off their branches and he paws a little circle clear at each base in thick mismatched gloves. He balls the cleared snow and he runs and throws it at the edge of the woods. He looks over the stream at the picture of the woods, brought out in high relief by the snow lying and hanging, frozen stuck on every branch, like the trees were lit from a thousand different places by something other than the sun.

Valentine's

You don't settle for long on the tills, not with tinned grapefruit being thumped under your nose. Dan blinks down at a stout woman in a clear plastic rain bonnet who, with a painful slow stutter, orders f-forty Carrolls and a t-t-t-two euro scratcher.

Make it a winner, she says.

Eliza the Hatter forgives Dan's daydream because he's a top-class communicator. The recipient of three gold stars in the Mystery Shopper reports. What can he say? He connects with the people. He can break them out of dead eyes, make them really see and hear him. Once they're paying attention, they're all smiles. Easiest is old women like Eliza. They're dying to smile at him. Then old men are second easiest. Joint third are middle-aged women and young children. They're both a bit stand-offish, both take a bit of work, but you can usually get to the mothers if you're civil to the wailing toddlers. Second hardest is girls his own age or a bit older and that's because of the potential for riding. The only ones who don't smile at all are men aged sixteen to sixty although some of the boys think about it too. It's because his time with the customers is short that Dan can safely make them love him. Eager to please, he's at his best with people he won't see again, gesturing and big eyes at the French camper van tourists who haven't a word of English. His pitch sharpening as he asks for their approval in language they don't understand.

Blazing charm is an interesting idea on Valentine's Day. Dan gets along rightly with a squint and a half-smile and a good pair of jeans but there's probably more to it than that. He does hide a serious quantity of jeans and shirts from Cahir. Shoes and hats and jackets. The delivery men have had to learn the safe spots in the shed, making dead drops inside the Christmas-tree box or under the empty coal bags, or in the zip-up compartment of Graham's golf bag. Fast fashion from overseas is not popular in the house and Dan has no good answer to Cahir's gurning about pollution and slave labour other than that's just how it works. Be shiny. Get the ride. You can't apologise for that. You have to make all common manoeuvres. He has to live. Jesus. Cahir would like it if Dan got all his clothes from the donation piles at the Good As New and he doesn't understand why Dan can't accept that. Dan will be coming into almost any room and Cahir will look him up and down and say, Is that new? Dan will tell him that actually it's organic and the factory is powered by windmills, so there.

Before Lydia, Dan's only other love was his second class

teacher, Muinteoir Lisa. She wore denim skirts with bare legs and polo-neck jumpers and she had the same shoes as his Auntie Patricia and everybody thought it was wile funny when he brought this up with Patricia. As if she could have thought she was the only one that had bought them in Christie's.

That's an awful tragedy, isn't it? Janine McGuinness says, pointing at the front of the *Inishowen Independent*. They were flying by all accounts, she says. The boy racers dead after a night at the Bailey.

It's desperate, says Dan. Like a waste, you know?

And they had a son hang himself too, the poor craiturs.

Janine loves to tell Dan that. She's steeped in misery. Some chronic but manageable diagnosis all that's between her and complete contentment. Dan stopped asking her How's things? once he learned how bad things could be. Janine loves the old tragedy, the new misery, the sad facts accumulating in a story. She has a chicken cooking in the deli, she says, but she wants to know if Dan can take for it now? She hands him a sticker for the half-price chicken, peeled from the plastic wrap, torn off the carcass. Janine is asking to have the two birds declared equivalent; raw and cooked. As if it hasn't been transformed in the oven. She wants to steal the cooking, the wages of the deli staff, a portion of their light, heat and power bill. Janine is betting Dan won't give her any bother and she's right enough. The surest quality of Janine's misery is that it spreads. He scans the label and asks her what time she's picking it up, then waits for her to get twenty cents out of her purse so she can save him on the change.

We only think we have troubles, ha? Dan says before she goes, knowing there's nothing Janine will hate more than having her relative fortune outlined. She makes a kind of questioning sigh like she would run them close and swings off with her bargain.

There is nobody in the chocolate-walled corral to keep Dan occupied and he wishes he had taken a stand against Janine and her poisons. The tenner she gave him was falling apart so he takes it back out for repair. Dan bites off a length of Sellotape and sets to the dextrous job of taping joints. Sealing the tear is an unavoidable intervention because an inert tissue will never heal itself and Dan doesn't want to leave the work to Lydia. It's a passable job when he's done and it might extend a lifespan. Cahir would like that Dan has an interest in repair. Dan's fingers have skill in them. They're quick and sure over the touchscreen buttons of the till, filing receipts and fishing for notes. He wonders was he too obvious at the end with Janine? He can use the wrong tone when thinking sincerely. The transit out of guff is an awkward shift.

Graham and Marie have been in a mud volcano. They rang to tell Dan about it and to ask how Cahir was doing. How did Dan think Cahir was doing? It's so annoying the way they do that. The way they talk as if Cahir is sick. Cahir is fine, he told them.

He steered them back to the volcano, which was like a

pyramid, they said, maybe fifty foot high, and they climbed up the side of it, to the rim, and then there was a stepladder leading down to the mud. Everyone was just climbing down, Graham said. And the mud was warm because it's connected to Hell, they said. It used to spew fire and lava and ashes until a young priest turned it to mud with some Holy Water and a prayer. Once they were in the mud, some local ladies started rubbing them without any warning, rubbing the mud furiously into their bodies, and the mud was so dense they could nearly float. Marie said she couldn't breathe with laughter and that was the main benefit of it. She couldn't remember a bigger fit of tickles since she was a child. When they were covered, they climbed out, heavy with muck, dripping, and they went to a lagoon where they were stripped and washed by another set of ladies, their swimming gear beat and wrung until the mud was gone.

Strangest afternoon in a long while, Graham said. What are you at this weekend? Any big dates?

The array of cut flowers is something to see. Pink and white and red. Pinky-red, orangey-red, bloody-red. Roses everywhere and they come with lilies, or tulips, or with a bit of greenery to bulk them up. There's a big stand of cards, robbery at three or four euro a pop, and teddy bears holding stitched pink hearts. I love you, they say. They still sell a bit of Milk Tray but it's not what it used to be. A box of chocolates bought on the way home from work is only for the long-suffering. An obligation fulfilled.

Dan does have a date with Amy the Rye but he doesn't care about that because the other night he got a picture of Lydia on a big white bed. She wasn't going out anywhere because she was getting old. She had to go to bed early even on Saturday nights. That's how she excused it, the two of them knowing rightly what she meant.

Mostly, Lydia's pictures aren't of white bedspreads or of herself. She sends Dan pictures of things. Or places. Or light. She's very good at taking pictures of the light, he thinks. Over the last month he's had a few snaps of a pockmarked concrete yard, of dead grass heads at the base of a rusting black gate, of a wooden coat stand and of the rough patches of plaster on the wall behind it. It's a room with a desk and a chair and some pencils in a glass jar. The jar is embossed with 'Churchtown Dairies' because they used to bottle milk on the farm, she says. She does sometimes answer his questions. She said she takes pictures and makes prints from them, or at least she used to. She said it like she was all embarrassed and Dan liked that.

He found an old page on the internet where Lydia had posted all the exhibition pieces from her degree show. The textured prints on lovely thick paper. Splatters and gouge marks. On Tuesday, after the gym, he went across to the shop and buzzed the cash office door. When Lydia let him in he almost chickened out. He started saying that he wanted to buy some sterling and did she know the exchange rate? When she was fiddling with the mouse and the keyboard, Dan found his nerve. Look at this, he said. He set his phone on her desk, the two of them shoulder to shoulder swiping through the pictures. Dan said they were so cool. He wanted to buy some of the prints. He said he didn't want to leave her short. They must be important to her. But if she could spare them, he would take *Comet* and *Creature*. Maybe *Crater* too. He said she had to name a price.

Lydia said he could have them all if he wanted. They weren't worth much lying in the shed.

That night, Lydia sent him a video. She was drunk, she said. Dan asked her for it. He said he wanted to see it. To see her. You're so beautiful, he said. So fucking perfect.

He didn't hardly get watching it. He was falling over himself to understand what he was seeing, to place her body on the bed. She didn't make a sound until it was nearly over. A short sigh. The video is gone but she sent it. She sent it at night when she wanted someone's touch. Good enough work for Valentine's Day.

Out of the Byre

C ahir is always on the road. Always walking. Molly's
Brae to Churchtown to Carrick and back. He walks for
hours at a time when Dan is at work and his old boots
are holding up rightly. In early March, the cows are out
in the swards closest to the Masters' farmhouse. Linked
to the byres by a gate and series of zigzag channels like
the queue lines at an airport check-in desk. Three mothers
and three calves, separated from the others, in a field opposite the Church of Ireland and its yellow crumbling wall.

Cahir stops to look at them. A spring calving suckler
herd, fluffy and brown in the sunlight. One of them is the
colour of golden fudge with a white face and big fudge spots
around her eyes, like birthmarks. One of them is ink black
and one of them is milk chocolate. Their coats are curly,
like baby bears, and they have yellow tags stamped into
their ear cartilage, for regulatory compliance. Nice wee

things. They definitely are. They'll stay where they are for now, until the calves are strong enough, and then they'll move out with the herd. To the dry parts of the farm that were closed first, where the herbage is already high. Then they'll move through the farm grazing everything. That's best practice. They'll stick with their dams until weaning and that means Cahir has a couple of months yet to be ready.

He has a new plan for a new grazing season. He is going to start using the Starlet. It's not ideal. But he has come to terms with it as the only way he can move things. He's going to get to know the cattle. He's going to placate them with the grass he cuts on Molly's Brae. He will use Graham's lawnmower and strimmer and he'll gather everything he trims. He has practised attaching the trailer to the hitch on the car and he will move the grass that way. He'll have to do it in the dark but that's OK. He'll dump the grass on the far side of their fence, and if their bellies are filled they'll have no need to invade. Hunger is a great driver of cruelty. They'll be much more amenable when full.

The days are starting to stretch. As everyone is so fond of noticing. You can't blame them for excitement. Everything is getting ready to stand up, open. Cahir is not many days away from knowing what he has. He thinks, he hopes, it really does look like they're all alive. They've passed every test. He keeps the penknife in the wheelbarrow and once a week he picks a bark to test. A light nick on the skin and every time green. Even the tiddler oak that was ripped out in the curling tongue. Even there, the buds are a little swollen, like they're being pushed open from the inside by something breaking out. The hawthorns he is sure of. Absolutely sure. Certainty is a new feeling for Cahir who has lived according to the rules he heard dispensed around him. Cahir stuck to the rules they gave him, glad of every new direction. Cahir stuck to every rule he ever heard but he never felt right until now.

He has ordered more stock. That's what he'll do next. Bare root so he can plant before dormancy ends. He's getting the ground ready in advance this time. Picking out the whin-bush seedlings. The coarse pricks yanked before they settle. They say the whins smell like coconut when they're in flower but Cahir has never smelt it and he's been close enough on his hands and knees. He's cutting back the brambles in doubled-up gloves. He cuts them short and then tries to pull them out. The newly rooted tips pull easily, but the established roots are hard to dislodge. He clears the soil as much as he can and he digs a gloved finger into the earth, following the branching strands and hooking under them, ripping them, tearing loose. Only when the smaller ties are snapped can he attempt to wiggle and pull at the central tap. The thick knotty core. The thorns are lethal and Cahir thinks blackberries are no forgiveness.

He'll get the next lot in the ground and then he'll move over the hill. To the high boglands. He'll find their family strip on the cutaway bog and dam the drains. Re-wet what is slowly drying out. Make it too wet again to cut or burn.

He thinks he might even go to the garden centre. That he might plant something in Graham's garden before he gets back. Nothing too ornamental or gaudy. You know. Nothing that's essentially sterile. Something that will help the birds or the flying insects.

A Second Planting

The new stock is delivered to the back door of the house in bags of water. The roots are still wet and the stems are in bud.

The second planting is much smoother than the first. Cahir has got himself a pitchfork and its sharp tines push easily into the earth, deep into the soil under whatever roots are bound there so that with only a bit of levering, Cahir can loosen and prise the grass roots in clumps. He can shred the clumps, ripping the fibrous associations apart and very quickly he has a hole to widen and shape with the spade.

Cahir has been reading up, learning over winter, and he has learned that his stand is too separate. That's not how they're growing above in the wood. The angles of inspection are irrelevant. What he needs is to create a huge entanglement of roots because it's the degree of connection below that will determine the success of the group. Standing as they are, little signposts on their own, they are too exposed to harsh climates. The storms that drive down into any gap in the canopy. The sun that bakes and dries the forest floor. It's the protection of the group that will ensure longevity. A second or third generation that might restore the earth to what it was before we cleared and burnt it. Before we dug up the corpses and burnt them too. The gnawed, subsumed bodies of older forests that were wasted deep in the cold and dark, concentrated, locked underground. Old woods that drowned and rotted. A deep important store. Cut, dug up, mined and burned. A whole world built on burning.

Cahir shakes a few mycorrhizal fungi in the planting hole, just a few granules into the bottom of each new hole. To waken the roots, to make them reach out.

Beside him, he has two bin bags full of leaf litter collected on the hill, teeming with complex forces too slow for him to see. A silent devouring, death and rot. The soaking wood chewed into mush, crawlies and fungus blooming on the sugary dew. A web of reabsorption. A dark, full world he can't remake. He filled the bags with the wet leaves and a few handfuls of musty soil, to nourish his own depleted ground.

Cahir builds a heavy layer of mulch around each new tree. There are seven more now, extending the copse nearer to the stream and he has placed them side by side. Oak with oak. Ash with ash. Holly with holly. Birch with birch. He plants them like with like because they can recognise their own. Because trees that are of the same stock benefit from growing close together. They don't compete. You'd think they would but they don't. They are careful with each other, with what space and light is already taken. Their crowns will stop short of crossing branches. They invest heavily in the success of the other because the day will come when they need the favour returned. They reinforce each other. They are partners and the partners are reluctant to let each other go. Sometimes they are so tightly connected at the roots, that their fates become entwined. Sometimes they die together.

Dinner and Drinks

What kind of a fish is ling do you think?

The waitress didn't take a drinks order and Sam is fit to be tied. He doesn't understand it in a good place like this. It's incomprehensible. It's a bad show is what it is. When they do get a couple of pints and a bottle of Rioja, the same girl comes back to say that, actually, they are out of the goats' cheese tart. She doesn't squirm or grimace. There is no attempt to soften the blow.

Lydia was excited to come. Everything is simple but expensively finished. The water has cucumber in it and the cutlery is shining in refracted candlelight, bounced by glass. The tables rise a grand hum. They booked a table as a birthday present to Lydia, even though the portions are generally thought to be small. Lydia feels responsible. She tries to pre-empt criticism of the service. To get ahead of it with a complaint of her own.

You wouldn't want to be hungry, she says.

I'm fine yet, Sam says, but Lydia can see that all the wheaten bread is finished and the butter pot is scraped clean.

Did you hear back about the paperwork?

Fucking solicitors, says Tom. I'm for the mad house. Everyone is agreed in principle. Even the ones on Molly's Brae, and that was some handling with them in Timbuktu or wherever. It's a pisstake. Making me hound and grovel for their magic gavel or wax seal or whatever.

When the plates do come, Tom tips his glass for another round. There are a few minutes of silence then until the hunger is blunted and they can return to politeness and offer swaps.

Do you want a mussel?

Try this foamy stuff. Oh, it's lovely.

Very tasty, I must say, says Dolly as they wrap their coats and scarves around them at the door.

They leave Dolly and the car in Churchtown and walk to the town. With Sam as cover, her and Tom can chance Pat's where the men crane their necks, thick and thin, as the door shakes in.

The silence lasts while the new round is ordered and the greetings are completed. Lydia is the only woman but at least she can sit in the main bar. It's a significant result for women's liberation because when Dolly and Sam were courting, Dolly had to sit in the kitchen and drink tea.

They are plunged into the middle of them. A private party of friends, technically open to the public but with very little sign of it over the door. They are getting warmed up, daring each other into well-worn positions. Pat gets them drinks and they sit down at a table below the bar. The high stools are all taken, varnished and black. Pat sets the glasses on stiff mats, no danger from the drippings, and pads the big square buttons of his till. Sam buys the first round. Lydia has a pint of Guinness with a dash of blackcurrant because Pat has the best of good Guinness.

The walls are panelled and painted all the way around and there is a replication toucan behind the bar. Carved mahogany rises behind the spirit bottles and the mirror stencilled with a thatched cottage. Pat laughs without smiling. Or his smile is too small to name. That's how they like him, her dad and the other men. A lot of blow-ins, a lot of individual men, teachers and guards and doctors and bachelors, coming for thirty or forty years, unironically drinking whiskey chasers with half-pints of stout. Pat shifts around like he's ignoring them, like he's furious they all came in to ruin his peace, but he never misses a drained glass. He sits on his stool a big, big man, and his face settles in a frown, an expert comic picking his bait.

You'd think they were a football team, he says finishing the previous conversation. I could get a team in here that would beat Dunree.

Lydia tenses when Sam throws into a story about the McLaughlins down in Malin, but they take him on like he's part of the general effort. Sam has a gentle air of seriousness; a hard-working man, lucky he was never refined.

The wedding cars were coming in the Lagg Road, Sam says, and all the horns were blowing, ribbons flying, and Sadie was stood in the yard watching them, waving and smiling out to them. When the last car was past, the sound of the last horn fading, Sadie turned to her sister Breege and she said, Hmpf, blowing for bother.

The men laugh at the two old spinsters and their funny lives, crouched on the edge of the world. Blowing for bother, ha?

But they had no value on marriage in that house, Sam says. None of them were married. Do you remember when Gerard was in here, Pat, with his lady out of the North?

Ms Rosamund Elliot. Pat sings her name with a trill. That was on the show day, he says. From Belfast. A divorcee too. We barely knew where to look with Father Morris in the corner. Bold as brass sucking Powers like it was their last night on earth. Waltzing in the marquee they were going. All we could wonder was how that top would hold her. 'We'll scare the wits out of them, Rosamund.' That's what Gerard said before they left. No doubt they did.

Brian McClure comes in full drunk, waving his arms, conducting, rousing them to derision and Pat to fury as he launches the chorus of 'Carn Fair'. When Brian tries a second verse they soon shout him down.

In the bigger crowd, they can't keep hold of one conversation and a raft of competing stories is in the air. As publican, peace commissioner and undertaker, Pat is talking to Bertie One Wing with professional certainty about the ascent of a drowned man from deep waters. A big, big place is the sea.

Lydia withdraws from the pain of a thing at its height. Them distilled, pot-bellied, light spilling around them. The clock beside the toucan says half-eleven. Pat should be stopped serving but they'll be going soon. Brian, the singing dose, is leaving and Lydia goes after him, past the boys telling about bitter tinctures of bogbine, out for a nip of fresh air in the inky night.

The wind is tearing cold from the north. Lydia wraps her coat tight and steps up and down the broad stones, avoiding the seams between. Alone without a sailing whirr or bumping lights she can't feel her own edges. They're smudged, avoided. She looks across at Fintan's. At the miniature hot air balloon in the window and the empty flower boxes on the second storey. The Diamond is planted with red roses under crab apples. Lavender and high grasses under multi-stem white birches. All of it is empty and bare. Disappointing. Lydia doesn't care if growth returns. That's the Guinness but it's the truth too. What the fuck is wrong with her? Why is none of it working? Tom and Sam and all the funny boys about the town. Congratulating each other on their shared heritage, their inherited history of the peculiar. This is what Lydia wanted so why is none of it right? She never thought they would disappoint her or let her down.

Lydia is full of an old wringing. An ache. She is bouncing with it. She came back because this was the last place she was strong and they were supposed to fix her and make her strong again but it's not working. It's not enough. She is balanced on the bricked edge, diminished, watching a man under a street light on Pound Street. Reeling but holding up, like he is hooked and caught, upheld by his string. He is waiting to be brought aboard, flailing, slapping, writhing to get loose from the line. He isn't risking a shout for all his desperation. Nothing that might scream on the tar or travel in the wind. He is looking for a solid thing to lean on, searching for a post with his hands outstretched and he falls to his knees looking for it.

Dan sent Lydia a picture earlier to wish her happy birthday. His shoulders were bare in it and his jaw was clean and pulled tight around his smile. She saved it even though he'll know that she did. And she came back to it again and again as she made herself come. Maybe he's in the town. In one of those other pubs. Dan wants to know her. He thinks she's worth something. Lydia handed the old prints over to him, like they were pieces of herself that she had disowned and he had recovered. Alone in the cash office where nobody can get in, Dan handled them like they were precious. Like he was afraid his hands were dirty and he should touch them as lightly and sparingly as possible.

He was saying thanks and telling her she had to start making stuff again. She was too good to stop. Lydia was reaching out to him, a fierce need to thank him, to please him. She had stepped right into him, so she was looking up into his face, searching his eyes and his lips when the buzzer for the door sounded. The harsh, grating buzz that wouldn't stop until she pressed the release button, until she let Veronica in.

Maybe Dan is the answer. Maybe they could go off together. Find some different life somewhere else. Maybe she only wants him for an hour. He might agree on her birthday. Lydia is fighting the ache, the drag. She is watching the man on the top street, bluish in his long coat, spewing on to the road. She can hear it pouring out of him, his back flinching with every churn and spill of boke as the rod is yanked. She blinks the water out of her eyes. Awake with the bite of the bitter air. He's on his feet again, shouting Fuck you! at whoever he sees coming out of the Park bar.

Him and His Dirty Surplice

B undled on the sofa in her wet gear, Lydia looks up to the door where Dolly is waiting for an answer. Should they go to Ballyliffin or Culdaff?

Lydia says she hasn't been to Lagg in ages.

In Churchtown, they are ten minutes from the sea. They'll get to it inevitably if they turn left at the gate. Lydia sits the Skoda between the big pillars and pulls carefully left and away from the yard. She stops at the white line of the junction. You wouldn't believe the speed they come round the corner at, getting away from the town and on to the road. Dolly's wee car is easy to slip round the Station Road, to squeeze over McSheffrey's Bridge and weave around the Malin Green. The rain is cleared but the tar is wet on the Lagg Road, a narrow path between grey water to the Isle and steep evergreen cliffs. The maroon hatchback in front is kicking up oily rainbows from something vital leaking on to the tyres and they follow that spray all the way to the wee church in the dunes, parking on a grassy flat area and forgetting to hold the doors when they get out into the gust. The grass is wiry and short. A tough squamous sort that grows only by the sea and which can take the weight of the cars easily. Walking a path under the obelisk headstones of the old graveyard, a few cows watch from the dunes and a black plastic bag, tattered on the barb wire, beats like a crow caught and thrashing, its throat torn to shreds. The cows are looking out at her. Happy on ground that can't last. The hills of sand and the chapel behind them are destined for drowning. Bit by bit they're eaten away.

Fine animals, Dolly says.

The entrance to the sand shifts with every angry lash. Every storm like a bomb smashing the path, leaving a bigger drop from the road. They go down sideways, stooped with one hand to the ground and they are alone and tiny on the flat at the bottom, in the shelter of marram hills slashed open at the seaside. The sand at the dunes is white and soft, deep and loose, but they walk further down where it's darker, firm and compact and where they can watch the weather in the stretching puddles, streamed over and over, washed up and washed away. The pebbles are grey, blue, peach, studded in the sand, and they try holding to what they can, they try to pin each new wave from retreat. The sawtooth sandy cliff tempts Lydia with scale and with a hollow where she could lie in the itchy marram cracks and pick grass to trace over her skin but she can't stop. She has to power on, trying to keep up with Dolly's tight clip.

164

She didn't tell Dolly about the man she found on his knees.

Lydia often hikes the hill behind Churchtown as a trick. To see if the trundling motion will pacify her and because Dolly says she is eating too much chocolate. Those Dairy Milk bars will settle somewhere and Lydia's wee frame won't suit the extra weight.

Cnocnacoilldara is the right name of the hill on a map. Hill of the Oak Wood. Lydia has never heard anyone use that name but she feels she should know these things when it drops and rolls to the bottom of their yard. The woods are old and ringed in heather but if you keep to bare paths you can reach the top easily and when you are high on the flank, you have a great picture of Sliabh Sneacht and of the mountain bogs. Lydia likes to stop at the fairy tree. She sits in the ferns until she is steady, under a stubby tree bent to one side like arthritic fingers, blown ragged and skinny by gales. She likes to count the chimneys burning, drifting smoke idly in calm, skyward scribbles.

At the top of the hill, a small iron cross stands upright in a mound of stones but Lydia took the lower path over the crest and down through the wood to Carrick. She wanted a quick look at Tom's new land. At the new arrangement of the hillside where he was setting up his perfect life. She was going to have another look at Bee's cottage. To compare it with Tom's plans and to decide if she should set up a meeting at the Credit Union and if that was a bad price to ward off ruin. Everything was still dead, the green withered rusty and crisp and Lydia timed her step down the hill to land on the crackliest heaps. At the Mass Rock, the ground is clear, flat and open under the massive canopy. With the leaves down it was like the roof had fallen in and Lydia worried that for any congregants, secret prayers might be riskier without a roof for cover. In the clearing, she wished she wasn't a godless cunt. That she could believe in things like Dolly or Sam. When Lydia sings at Mass she only wonders how they got such high ceilings through a budget committee. She only sniggers at them sticking out their grainy tongues to take Communion. A prayer would be nice, probably, for the beat as you ran through as much as any hope it's heeded.

She was breaking a sweat down her back and a shake through her thighs as she skipped downhill, struggling to stay in charge of her own momentum. She was coming to the edge of the woods, through the clearing under the altar, where the trees end at the rocky stream, where the fields are small and ill-defined, bleeding into each other, and where she doesn't know who owns what, only that Tom will soon own it all. She almost tipped over when she saw him.

Kneeling alone in the middle of the field opposite her, hooded and bowed in a navy overcoat, it was hard not to run into view. Lydia pulled back and waited, hidden by the evergreen of the holly trees and the tumble of thorned brambles. She thought of a fox hunter or rabbit courser, but on his knees with his hands at the earth, he looked more like a prospector, like he was sifting the muck for precious or semi-precious materials. There was a wheelbarrow to one side of him and a spade resting forenenst it. It wouldn't

166

be Tom or any of the boys about the farm. Not in a big woollen coat.

Lydia was surprised at the fear that poured through her for the shovel at his hand. She was afraid of how fast she could run in welly boots and tight jeans. Her breath was so loud and she was furious with it. She tried to think about Tom or her dad or even Dolly. Practical people who would be calm and who might want her to have proof before they compiled a plan of action. All Lydia could do was fiddle with the lens on her camera, adjusting the zoom and focus, trying to amass evidence.

There was a bare stalk of about three foot. That's what his hands were at. He traced each part of it, inspecting top to bottom, reaching back and forth to the wee bucket beside him and to a green watering can. When he got up to wipe his hands on his bum and his thighs and trail his cuff across his forehead, his eyes tilted up and he put his hands out into the air, like he was dizzy and might fall. Lydia knew Cahir's untidy face immediately. His thick neck and coarse features.

It was a relief to have his specific name. Cahir is a word something like inert. Lydia watched him walking, taking his implements with him, then kneeling again to pull at grass with his fists, tracing different parts of each new stalk, bent close to see them. He moved very carefully, respectfully, and he was singing. In the quiet, his song drifted up like the chimney smoke, generally upward and dispersing. Life was back beneath her, dissociated, and she was able to tweak and tilt it. To make a fine assembly of rushes and piled roots, of spires and chimneys, and Cahir, dwarfed by the island piles of tidied scrub, wood dying in different ways. Kneeling there on the slope like a wee boy in prayer, wiping his dirty hands on his brow and on his tattered surplice.

Could you not stay in for a ween of days, Lydia? You're sniftering there. You should go into Borderland and get one of those puffy coats.

Lydia says nothing to Dolly about Cahir and the trees. On the beach at Lagg, she doesn't mention the scar, the great white rupture of the ridge or that this would be the best place to walk into the sea. You can't swim in these waters. There are terrible currents and warning signs everywhere, none as good as the shipwreck poking up at low tide.

This water is not for swimming. It's for reminding Lydia of what she owns. This is her sea. These lying waters, cursed burial ground of gods, they crash and break for everybody but the shifting bed, the encroaching, rubbling depths are Lydia's only. Sam's family lived on the Isle of Doagh before they moved to Carn. They are seven or eight hundred years between the two places, only a few miles apart. A collection of low thatched cottages above the castle and the stony swing of Pollan Beach, they lived on the Isle until the dunes made it impossible to stay. Until a storm buried what they owned in sand. Not far from the land they abandoned, flat stones are marked in cups and rings, like drops of rain fell too heavy and cut their way into the rock, marking entry with a notch and ripples. A picture of a very heavy rain or a group of stars. A way of speaking we can't understand.

In no time the sky is full and getting dark and she thinks Dolly says, Oh we'll be soaked, but she can't be sure with Dolly's voice carried off like a tissue in the wind.

Everything turns grey and they can do nothing but keep going. They've made the turn and there is no quicker way back. The stones crop up smooth as silk, rounded and curved by attrition into the hump of a barrel, or the stump of a great stone tree, like acid-washed denim streaked with white from the bleach. They keep going, a bit faster but wet already and the rain is passing in the gusts. Round under Knockamany, they come by the back of a stone cavalry, cragged and black, marching up the beach from the water, spiked peaks stuck with shells, twisted like the spires of a foreign empire. That's where her and Tom used to pick winkles when they were little, fighting to see who had the most, Dolly weighing the buckets by hand and declaring no winners. Lydia doesn't know if she remembers the day itself or only the picture of them in their wee raincoats and their red boots, and she doesn't know if it matters.

On their way back, every air blasts at them, wet and bitter, and the bands of flat colour are running with wisps and swirls, sloughing particles to spin in the roar. It only took twenty-five minutes. Twenty-five minutes spent at the edge and end of any attempt. The limit where they meet what's inhuman. It's only a ten-minute drive from the house and they only went because they had two scones each with their tea and here it is. The lash of forces that exist without them, making things that are huge and indifferent to the two of them scurrying out the road with no sign of the Charolais cows, trying to hold their hoods up until they reach the car.

Tax Credits

L ydia boils the kettle and makes breakfast tea, weak with
lots of milk and one sugar. Dolly's wheaten bread is cut
thick and the fridge is raided for the rest. A bowl of boiled
eggs, tomatoes on the vine, a block of white cheddar and a
hunk of butter in the dish.

I can't see the ham, Mum.

Did I not buy ham? I swear I did, says Dolly. I asked
Sandra to cut me five thick slices of Grant's ham. She comes
to double-check the fridge. For God's sake, we're all losing
our minds. We'll make do without it because I'm not going
back down.

The thing is, Lydia isn't motherly. Even if she had a
wee Christmas baby like Aoife Harkin, it would be
a disaster. She's too selfish to have a baby. She always
wants to be on her own in a way that's very unhelpful for
rearing children. She could manage the clinking crystal

and a song at the piano. She could learn to be a host, but she'll never be a mother. She is stunted. She's only ever birthed some pockmarked metal, hidden over in the shed, swaddled undercover. She's sterile and perfect where it should be messy and warm.

Tom says you have to start a pension by the time you're twenty-five. Compound interest is magic, he says.

Maybe Lydia could make herself. Maybe she could go and study primary teaching and learn Dolly's recipe for pancake batter. Teach the kids their prayers and how to look contrite for their Holy Communion. She could be financially viable teaching best behaviour for the bishop and weaving St Brigid's crosses. Walking up the Church Road with the whole class to get their ashes for Lent. She could learn enough piano to accompany Christmas plays and she mightn't mind the evenings spent alone.

How did she never think it through? That none of them are here for her convenience. For when she's had enough of silence. That she can't be part of a family if she brings nothing to it. That families are child-rearing enterprises. And Tom and Ellen will be the heart of hers. At the periphery, she'll need something of her own.

In the Good As New shop, Lydia needs to see Cahir up close. To face him properly with what she knows. Her new appreciation of him as the smiling man in Dan's pictures, the singing man on mucky knees. Cahir is sitting at a table inside the door, facing down the Malin Road. Lydia thought he might panic. That he might get up and hide.

But he barely looks at her. After waving hello he sits at his desk, head down, teasing out the end of a blue rope.

Lydia smiles and has a gander. At the cacti in ceramic pots and the Boston ferns in ruby glass bowls, waving feathery, glinting kitsch from the concrete and bare sanded wood. It doesn't smell like the other Good As New shops.

On a cork board behind his desk there are explanatory notes. One of them says, *Thank You for Supporting the Circular Economy!* and another says, *All funds from our current collection are for the Carndonagh Parish.*

On one shelf there are a series of small plastic blobs and a stiff card claiming them as *Hand Crafted Ducks. Made from plastic recovered at Pollan Strand.*

They don't look like ducks.

On a clothes-line strung between two metal rails, a bunch of scarves are hung with wooden pegs and Lydia picks one. Blue and green silk like a tropical jungle. She's delighted to find something she likes and as she approaches the desk Cahir puts down his length of rope.

Hi, Cahir! Lydia gives her warmest smile, eyebrows up. How much for this? Scarves are ten euro, he says.

It's really lovely, Cahir. The place, I mean. I can't believe I've never been in before. Is it all donated?

Yeah, he says. Thanks. We get heaps in but it's rubbish mostly. Stuff they were too ashamed to send to the wee black babies.

Lydia laughs nervously but Cahir seems happy with his joke. She checks his hands. Eager for evidence of his other work, glad to see them covered in little cuts and that the thumbnail of his left hand is holding dirt. Lydia forgot that he doesn't like to look you in the face. It was the same in school. Like he was embarrassed, always looking down and away from her, always with quick small steps, like he was on his tiptoes, like he was waiting to bounce away. Lydia was relieved when he was moved, even though he let her copy his notes, because it was unnerving how quiet he could be, how he was so obviously watching everything she did but with his head always down. People said he went mental before the exams. Schizo they all said. Some sort of break in himself. Lydia doesn't know if that was true.

She has been all day in the milkshed, cold seeping from the plaster walls. The electric heater at her feet. Wrapped in big jumpers and a scarf. She is through most of the day without sharpening up, unaware of herself, a loose blur with no proper edges and she drew things and wrote things she had never thought of and can hardly remember. She made sketches of the island piles of rotting wood, the wooded slope and rocky stream, the town on another hill in the distance. Drawing him, trying to capture the discomfort in his shoulders, the resolute smallness in his hands, held together.

It's nothing to do with her. It's his odd impulse she wants committed to paper. Him himself. Living off scraps. In a corner that he thinks is his. What he thinks is secret. That he doesn't know is all for nothing.

Coming back over to the house and helping Dolly set the table for dinner, Lydia is drained, perfectly drained. Like every need in her body is expressed, every attention given. Empty, and it feels so good she can hardly take it.

Link Box

M um, can I take the piano to Carrick?

Dolly looks up from her crossword. God, she says, are you going at last? Her smile is full of expensive crowns and her tone is mock surprise but she doesn't fool Lydia.

I don't know, Lydia says, I'll follow the piano I think.

Did you hear there's a quiz in Murphy's tonight for one of the Breslins in Cloontagh. Their hay barn burned to the ground because one of the young fellas tried to torch a wasp's nest. They're not half right, that crowd, says Dolly. Rotten with money though.

Can I take the piano then?

I'll get Tom to leave it out tomorrow. Will you be about to help?

It's easier done than Lydia feared. Donal is helping Tom in the yard and it takes only half an hour to move the piano on the back of the tractor. In a link box lined with old duvets and Tom standing on beside it. Dolly said the duvets were worn thin and that after as many years it was no shame for them. The piano sits on iron casters and after being lifted over the threshold, it rolls into the musty hall.

When Tom and Donal are gone, Lydia opens the lid on the piano stool and sifts through the music, loose pages with pencilled instructions over the chords. She takes out an old book wrapped in brown paper. On the inside page, *Bridget Doherty* is written in fine cursive hand. Lydia sits and plays a few bars of a waltz, right hand only, trying to count out the beats and hear the tune, and then she puts the book away under a box of yellow blessed candles, compressed, immured, where it'll survive for another time. When she's putting it back she finds a sheet of handwritten tongue-twisters and says them aloud.

How much wood could a woodchuck chuck.

Betty bought a bit of butter.

Peter Piper picked a peck of pickled peppers.

She says them all a few times, tripping here and there and then files that away too. She doesn't want to rouse an old stutter.

She lights a fire in the iron grate and it splits and cracks and the keys in the doors work as they should. They even hang on their own set. It's not grand like what Tom will build. It's not perfect and it will need a lot of work but the garden can be lovely and it will open out on to the Well Field that runs up toward the woods. She can have all that space. Lydia walks back home before bedtime because she has no bed in Carrick. She'll have to start calling it something other than home. Churchtown is what other people call

Dolly's house. Lydia walks back to Churchtown and she thinks that the sitting room looks empty and asymmetric.

Everyone is out and Lydia isn't boiling spuds for herself. She whips three eggs in a glass bowl with a fork, stringing the yolks through the white, pouring them over the fried tomatoes. She scatters the top with cubed Feta and puts the pan under the grill so the eggs fluff up. There is a stoppered bottle of Shiraz beside the kettle and she pours a glass. She eats her eggs from the pan, splotched with mustard, brave with the piano moved, and because of her new idea. Her expanding view. It is no longer solely about the figure on his knees. That's not enough for an image of reality. She is going to collect what she can from the slope. Every picture and weed that will show them Cahir's act. Today, she printed an OS map of the site. She enlarged it at the Council Offices and she has marked the boundaries of the site in red marker. The field that will soon be Tom's. She cleared the walls of the milkshed so that there is space to pin up the sheet and much more too.

Dried foxglove
Hawthorn flowers
Oak leaves and acorns
Pressed ferns

Lydia makes a list in her head of what she could collect through the year and hang in the small shed. She lists anything she could grind and paint with. She found a printmaking workshop in Derry and paid a fee to use their presses under supervision.

Vibrations run through her. Tiny tremors in her muscles that can't be stretched away. Pushing through the covers, cocking her heels and wrists away from her, scrunching up. It takes Lydia a second to remember that it's Monday and that she is on holiday. One of four mandated weeks' holiday. She has all week to be with herself in the shed. The sun is coming in the crack of her curtains and she remembers nothing of the night. Stretching hard, Lydia is happy to have a day here bounded by the sea and the small roads that lead to it. She is happy again imagining the dark hedges that surround her cottage garden and what's growing there. What'll soon flower on her verge.

Determination is shooting through her, growing minute by minute, like a rush. Vigorous and ineradicable. She takes a daily Polaroid of every tree and she can see them on the walls, coming into bud. She is going to etch the buds and run ink into the indents on the copper. She is going to sift through the big piles of old roots. The bushes that were cut and heaped. She is going to make woodblock prints of Cahir and his trees and anything else she can. A man at the workshop in Derry says he can carve them for her. The thought of it, whispered to herself, brought tears that wet her lips and were tangy on them.

She is a new woman since she started choosing what should be carved into the wood. She is washed down in every fold and crevice, hummed out clean. Like she is properly oxygenated for the first time. Like she can get her first deep breath in years. Now that she's invincible, she can be happy for Tom. She will enjoy every minute of the run in. She will walk the aisle smiling, submit to every choice and delight in the fruit cake composition, the chocolate butter-cream, and the sturdiness of the cake construction. She will listen to the list of harpists and laugh at the names of prospective cocktails. She will dream in harp and cello and love Ellen when she sees her in her simple dress and her trailing lace veil. The lightness and simplicity of it a great let-down for the spectators in the back pews but precisely what was meant.

She puts on her wellies at the back door, bunching her pyjama bottoms around her ankles and slipping into the boots, toe-first, like into a glass slipper. In Cahir's field, Lydia walks the line he walks, making notes. Until the leaves burst, she can't guess the names. At the top of the slope she is nervous for them. They're too small. Just one stalk each, a pencil thick, in a small pool of black soil and the weeds and rushes grown up as high as them, not far away. Her boots squelch on the clipped stubble around each tree. Where he has cut a ring with his shears. It must be hard work because there is only a small circle cleared round them. She walks in the genuine gold of the sunlight, pooling and shifting over her slow march, her procession. She picks at the grasses as she goes, running her hand through the prickly tops and pulling the softer ones to run through her fingers. Life is coming in a flood and it's holding. A familiar gloom reached out to her and she welcomed it, spiteful, reaching back toward the pain. Now, it flees at her gaze. Dolly tells Lydia all the bars from the town and she laughs. She sniggers at Tom coming into the yard. The sound of his wee car through the sitting-room window, sailing through the narrow gate and round to the back step. First a bit fast, then carefully, growling like their old ride-on lawnmower. The land is still not bought, he says, and Lydia hopes for more delay.

Silver Circle

By the end of April, urgency is in the air and the milk-shed walls are full. The buds have burst and they are plastered everywhere. The wheelbarrow is shot from every angle. She photographs the tip of the spade and the dried muck on the trowel and the old blade of the shears. Lydia works in the shed every morning and then goes to count money in the cash office or back to sleep. She's up first thing, cockcrow, the creaks of dawn, without giving herself room to dither or escape. She works out the notes from the day before and in the process makes more. She likes to sit in the lower sitting room afterward in fits of dozing before waking as if for the first time.

She finds herself planning the garden in Carrick and Dolly's decisions no longer break her heart. At the back, there will be a big run of grass to the tree boundary. Switch grass and purple moor grass, black flowered mountain grass and North American prairie grass. A rising series of banks that will rustle and bust into the wind. Airy meadows falling from her front door, too light and individual to stagnate, get soggy, or rot. High, like a July road verge, a sort of Eden in abundance. Then birch, she thinks, and something evergreen. Honeybees and bumblebees but not a hive straight away. Days and days given to potting and pruning and planting. The rhythm of the perennials, the spring of new bulbs. In the meadow, at the back, she will throw the seeds and see what comes. In time she might learn what makes a living thing grow. She is keeping the foxgloves and the honeysuckle through the hawthorns. Her granny in Effish was famous for a foxglove poultice, crushing the oils into glass bottles, an expectorant of all ills. Fairy's glove, withdrawer of poison. They say she used the dried leaves as snuff she was so inured. Lydia is planning a general sanctuary for more than bees. Yesterday she made a list of butterfly-friendly bushes.

She brings Tom a cup of tea and starts giving out.

Did you see they've set up a car wash round the circular road? They're pouring suds into the river. Is there, I don't know, an Environmental Protection Agency or something?

Or something, he says. Tom looks up from his phone. It's the wild, he says. Did you not know? People here don't believe in the state.

Dolly comes in and Lydia asks her if she believes in the state.

I believe we need to get the dinner on, Dolly says.

Poundies for the people! There's a creed to live by. Tom is standing, pulling on his trainers. Happier the closer life gets to being a joke. Now you're both here, he says, I'm supposed to tell you that Teresa the Mean is booked for the wedding and you both have to do a trial in two weeks.

Oh shit, says Lydia.

What?

Her stuff is very glam.

Don't make a fuss, Lydia. She's Ellen's friend. I'm sure she'll do you up as plain as you like.

After the tea, Dolly starts making scones. Just to soothe herself. Not because they need them. Lydia walks outside barefoot on the concrete, and steps lightly as far as the grass, which is damp from yesterday's rain. Long ago she was taught to go easy by hard landings and the scream of her arches.

The daisy hearts dye her toes yellow and she isn't happy. Nothing is purged. She is not in ecstasy or high spirits. It's something much better than that.

It is the first day that makes Lydia consider hoovering her car. The first warm day. Everything is yellow. It sprouts in lines on every lane where the whins, bright as Colman's Mustard, line fields and clump on hill faces. She snatches a whiff of cut grass. She wakes up in daylight and will soon sleep in it too. It's hard at first to close her eyes against the opportunity of a bright evening. Lent is almost over and Lydia forgot to deny herself. She is away from the shed on errands, collecting money for Dolly's Silver Circle. In flying form. Giddy. Fearless.

Tonight they are singing at Holy Thursday mass. A record

183

late Easter. 'Adoramos Te' and 'Pange Lingua', parading round the church aisles. It's a whole palaver with Father McDaid coming behind them in a fringed shawl under a white canopy hoisted by four men. Four of the same men who had their feet ritually washed. Glaring white and pre-washed feet, pulled from reluctant socks. The full show of power will be out. A double-digit team of altar servers in ivory cassocks, one scattering scented smoke from the thurible to roll high into the spotlights, higher and higher toward the painted hearts, red and circled in thorns. She can smell it drifting, shook, fed with every silver spoonful on to the coals.

Incense drifts with Lydia as she climbs the white stairwell at the shop. Her holiday week is nearly over and she needs to check the rota.

At the top of the stairs, coming past the silver doors of the lift, she hears a metallic smash and someone shout, Fuck!

The door of the Good As New is open and John is in the middle of the floor, surrounded by disposable coffee cups. He sees her.

Lydia? Thank God, he says. Come here quick. Come in here. John ushers Lydia into the room and closes the door after her. She can hear the door lock.

I broke some wee bird, John says. It was hanging up inside the door. That's it there look, all over the floor. John holds her arm, at the elbow like before. He sees the card in her hand and asks: What's that?

I'm selling Silver Circle lines for Mum, Lydia says. They are trying to clear the debt in the hall. Ninety thousand it was last year but they're hoping this drive will clear it.

Lydia suppresses a smile as John drops her arm, hesitating. They don't move apart. Their bodies are physically close. Near enough to feel a beat drubbing. John bows his head, breathing her in.

Standing close to him, Lydia finally sees the boy she knew. Close to her body like this, John is the boy in the cold shade, on the gravel path, and she is flinging adoration at his feet. Like it was nothing to be loved.

John does want her. She was wrong. He was trying to hold apart but he can't any more. They're too close. He's waiting for a sign that she wants him too. A thrill surges in Lydia, like a little girl at the top of a very high slide, sitting on the edge and one small move is all it will take to send her rushing away. Like she's not big enough or old enough to be here. Like she somehow slipped past the steward and she has to take her chance now before someone catches her and makes her stop.

On the bare concrete floor, scattered with compostable cups and metal pieces, John wants her so much. That means Lydia can take his body and fix everything. The mistakes she made can be erased. Everything she spat at can still be hers. Everything she was too good for. Not good enough for. Lydia can be the girl that John adored. The meaning of the past changes as they pull close together and their lips meet, just barely, before pulling back like from a first kiss.

Are you sure? John asks, no trust yet in his eye.

Lydia kisses him back, not softly, moving toward him as if their bodies aren't solid. As if the kiss has made their frames passable and they could get closer than side by side, both responsible for the fractures. It'll be bits and pieces every way they try and do it, even if they stop and go for the dustpan. They keep going. Trampling over the jigsaw pieces of the broken sparrow, dull mirrors bouncing a fraction of incident light, shifting the pieces from where they fell and lay as if they could be put back together or remade whole. They are on the soft blanket and on the green chair, trying to extend themselves. They are shifting, smiling, serious enough, leaning on anything solid. Trying to bring each other up into heating skin. It's a short effort of spit and eager breathing until John comes and they're back above the scattered mess, partners again.

Lydia fixes herself on a side table, fiddling with a lacquered box. Eastern-looking, full of old beads and tarnished metal, bracelets and brooches. She smoothes out her dress, wriggling her toes inside her runners. She checks the green velvet armchair for stains. John is delighted with himself, doing up his belt and she doesn't blame him. Fucking in a big glass box above the town. The sight lines to the road completely untested. Lydia takes a scarf from the clothes-line and tells John to clean his mess.

I'll stay and talk to Cahir, he says.

They kiss another time and Lydia leaves whispering to herself, the girl who will have everything, happy that John is going to pay up. Somebody should. If he's going to pay for the smashed bird and the dirtied scarf, he could have bought a few lines of the Silver Circle too, she thinks. Her card is nearly full and it's three lines for a fiver.

Grazing

This morning there were over forty hairs on Cahir's pillow. He picked them one by one from the cotton-polyester blend so that he could examine the white bulbs and heap them together to be flushed. The toilet is the safest place to dispose of body parts. On Friday he lost a hundred and seventy-five hairs in the shower. He teased them from the clot in the drain guard and counted them. This last day or two he can't touch his head without shedding and that's how quick things can turn. A man's hair can fall out of his head before he's even finished putting himself together. Him not ready for exhibition and skipping on to disintegration. Nothing left to discover except the extent to which his genes are inviolable and it's not an important discovery, that he's pure human.

It's not a theory about the evening star. It's not proof that the stars can't be swept or tossed or prayed on. It only shows how quick and easy we fall apart and Cahir adds it to the list of things he knows. Cahir knows that nothing good can dare be delicate. That silvery-looking sparrows can't stay in the sky.

Cahir has to keep old discoveries close. Discoveries that are only partly his, like John Glen was always a dickhead. He was always pretending to be reasonable at the back of the group that held Cahir down, on the edge of the gravel, pinned to the grass with their knees on his straining chest. Feeding him tufts of grass, ripped out in handfuls and shoved into his mouth. John never did any of the feeding. He never made any of the drawings, just laughed as they passed them along and there can't be a crime in laughing when someone is so funny-looking. Such a wrong shape. Everybody was laughing, even Cahir, and laughing is like consent. John paid Cahir a hundred euro for the sparrow, which is much more than it cost him.

Listen, I'm wile sorry, John said. I tripped and banged into the door and the wee bird fell down from the roof. I hope you can get another one, he said, as he handed Cahir the money. As he bet on the soothing sight of two fiftys folded over.

Cahir was just hoping that laughter would make them stop. He didn't know any other way. Not when they were holding him down. Not when they were shouting about him in the corridors, about how he wouldn't go to the showers after PE.

These things happen, John said.

John is so easy to like. Laughing along, kicking about, making no fuss. He was always well got. Prince John coming into his kingdom and who would deny such a nice lad? So personable and sweet-natured. So down to earth even with all the things he owns. Cahir would just like to see some fairness. Some sort of penance for the structures they've created. The comfort of a five-year projection, the power of wealth swelling as debt is paid and profits rise, it should cost more than an accountant's fee. Cahir wants John trapped in the Health and Wellness aisle, longing for the promise he exchanged, sunk into the tarmac, swallowed by the weight of the place. Torn down to the dirt by 25,000 square foot of concrete and steel, dragged under, gasping against the clay and the grass in his mouth and his nostrils, wriggling and crying and wishing *he* could be dead. Knowing that it's too late for longing. The big numbers are heavy and they've lulled him in and they should sink him step by step but they won't.

The morning and the evening star are the same star and they're not a star at all. The sparrow fell when John dropped his box of coffee cups. These are old and new discoveries.

Cahir slices the sod with a spade, sweating over weeds and the widening of dark defences. In suppression of ferns and dock leaves, nettles and rushes. All the buds are open.

Mayday

Noise is ringing from the Diamond on what is Carn's only parade. The brass band is marching with the cornets in front, gleaming gold, and the lines of players, tall and short, are proud to be honking in their yellow ties, to have the tricolour fluttering. It's 'Amhrán na bhFiann' that Cahir can hear as they pass the Council Offices. They're ringing it carefully from their cheeks, rough at the final discordant phrases. If he moved closer to the window Cahir would see the parade march the ring road but he knows the shape of it without looking; the civil defence force and the accordion band, sports clubs and rally cars, a few men in drag throwing sweets and soapy water.

Cahir stays sitting with his book where the heroine is measuring her lovers. She has already spurned a monkish man. One of those serious, academic men. A proud defender of good and steady character presented innocently without even a wanking habit. Cahir imagines Mr Boldwood can only come if he's looking at himself in the mirror.

Cahir has had a hectic day and he knows he should be happy. He should be grateful, not mad. He knows it's wrong to be so mad but he can't help it sometimes. Six of them didn't buy a fucking iota. They just ran their dirty paws all over his denim shirts. They were such a bad cast of faces too. A bit deformed and all unfinished like first attempts in a beginners' pottery class, lumps of clay barely pressed into recognisable form, their identifiable features hardly outlined by thumbs stuck too heavily in all the wrong places. With the steps on the stairs, Cahir has to be ready. He is arranging his face until he hears Dan shout out, Hello!

Dan is finished his shift and dying from the Bank Holiday pints but Cahir can't look too happy to see him. He has to think of the vomit.

Early in the morning, with Dan gone to work, Cahir sponged it over and back on the laminate boards until it soaked away. He wrung it from the J-cloth into the drains because he was afraid it would soak into the wood. A viscous, acidic soup that would eat into the boards. When most of it was in the bin, he mopped the floor to lift the leftover skim. Why can't Dan hold himself together? It's those silly wee pricks he goes around with. The one with the Audi. And the other one. Making so much noise getting ice from the freezer, shouting without a thought for what choices harden or fix.

Listen, before you start, Dan says, pleading, I'm at death's actual door. OK? Actual death. Me at the door. And I never buy plastic. Dan is carrying a bottle of Lucozade Sport and a roll from the deli wrapped in branded greaseproof paper.

Cahir should have worn gloves to separate his finger-nails from the absorbent cloth. It would have protected him a little.

Dan sits on the green velvet chair, knees together, his white ankle socks in view. He opens his roll and Cahir wants to snap at him. To protect the green velvet. To check his fingers for mayonnaise and grease. Dan was wrong to make a mess and Cahir needs to correct him. To make it right again. So that both of them are clean and right.

I'm sorry about the vomit, Dan says. I know I need to cop on. No more body fluids on the floor, I promise.

Dan is like a wee boy saying sorry, head bowed and knees pressed together, trying to balance the crusty roll on his lap. Cahir believes him straight away. He sinks down, relieved he didn't spit abuse or accusation. He has had bad news already.

Did you hear Matt McHugh killed himself?

Jesus Christ, says Dan, his mouth full of spicy chicken and coleslaw. Would you let me get a bite?

Matt was tiny, like a matchstick man, and now he's hanged himself over a gambling debt they're saying. The same oul shite. Happy as Larry, he was. A lovely young fella! The word is that he was right and drunk, but nothing out of the ordinary.

I'm very sorry about Matt.

That's what Cahir would have to say to the family. Him spinning on the spot wondering who was immediate family and who was just making sandwiches. If they're not standing around the coffin he won't know whose hand to shake. Matt was always very nice, he could say. We once co-delivered a PowerPoint presentation. Matt was very conscientious about research. Would that be too insignificant a detail? A memory of that goodness can't have been enough for Matt and Cahir can't tell what hate or pain he's had since, what made him hang himself in the same house as his family with his shirt-sleeves torn off and stuffed between the rope and his neck.

Anyway, it's not a sin now, just a fucking disaster. He has a wee boy, they're saying, only two or three years old and all the pictures are of him. Everybody is leaving messages to the dead man and Cahir wonders if the Blessed Virgin has access to Facebook comments. He wonders will they show his wee son the made-up body? The job done to hide violence. The white frilly silk, and the pool of Mass cards, and the pictures of him and his friends, him and his wife, him and the wee blond boy?

Matt couldn't take it. He got over the first scare of clarity and things weren't getting any better. The pain wasn't going away. Unpicked and restitched. Too far down one road and not fit for coming back. Or maybe he was just off his face. They say he went mental on the drugs. Lines of this, that, and the other. In the fucking K-hole or something. Few yokes and a drop of acid. Chewing your jaws off beside some young one and getting her up the duff.

Dan is opening the lid of his fizzy orange. The plastic seal cracks and hisses. Were you talking to Mum and Dad? he asks. Where are they now?

Cahir itches his scalp, trying not to shake anything loose. He tries to focus on the question.

El Chaltén, he says. Fairy-tale mountains. Sharp icy peaks. And they went and saw the calving glaciers fall into the sea and I told her she can thank her long-haul flight for that opportunity.

Fuck sake, Cahir. She'll be trying to come home by boat now. Dad will kill you if she cancels the flight.

Serves them right. I told her that travel is the last refuge of boring people. But, at the same time, maybe they should chance another few miles when they're so far down. They'll not get the opportunity again. No sense turning for home yet, I said. What about Antarctica?

Dan snorts. I'm actually jealous of Patagonia, he says. And Buenos Aires.

Cahir takes his pulse until the resting beat is restored. He won't go to the wake. Dan wouldn't come with him and he couldn't walk in alone. Nobody will care if he goes anyway. He looks at Dan and forgives him for the vomit. Just don't kill yourself. OK? Whatever you do. Just keep away from the K-hole and whatever else might draw you to a snuffing out. Cahir will collect plastic bottles for the two of them. He'll refashion it somehow, the faded jetsam. Slice and glue it with hairless fingers.

He should be telling Dan about the trees. He said he would do it when they were living and unrolled. Not yet, he said, when they were almost there, half open, green and tinted red at the edges. Not yet when he had the hawthorns. Still not yet when he had the birches because he was waiting on the oaks. Oaks were slow to come and it would be nothing if they weren't alive and green. He wanted to point at the giants in the wood. He thought

195

that would make it clear. He'd say that the root of the word used for oak is the same as the root of the word for truth. He would take Dan for a walk in the greenish shade of the woods and point out the damp growth. He'd explain how special and rare it was. How, as the owners, they were responsible. How with active management they could protect and increase the good. The two of them, together.

He planned the talk he would give as he watched the oak buds open. Darker and brassy at the node, turning golden as they lengthened, the green coming out at the tip of the spear, a bulge that messes clean lines, a serrated unfurling of coral, popcorn skin covered in downy white hairs like a baby. He picked his words as he listened to the birdsong, as he knelt close to the wet spiderwebs, stretching between slender limbs, raindrops hanging on the undersides.

Cahir's hands are unsteady and there is no hope of going back to Bathsheba. Looking at Dan scrolling his phone, his clear complexion numbed and flattened, Cahir wants to shout before it's stolen away. He wants to explain himself to the only person he could possibly tell but the thought of the words coming out his mouth brings a tremor into Cahir. A vibration that starts small and neat but which widens into a jerking sawing wave until his whole body is shaking, and he knows he can't say it. He can't let any little part go, not to anyone, because he doesn't know what Dan would say. He doesn't know which bits and pieces are structural or load-bearing. The parts that are essential for holding together.

Did you know, he says, that the Great Wall of China is held together by sticky rice?

Cahir, that's racist, says Dan, the words garbled by the half chewed end of his roll.

No, seriously, Cahir says, I read it somewhere. Three per cent mixed in with lime and it's stronger than modern mortar, they say. An organic bonding agent the same as what's inside bones.

Firebrand

The wind is slapping the windows, rippling the hedges with slanting blows as light is thrown past. Cahir is hoping the wind will blow water from somewhere or that it might dislodge the blocking fronts because they are crying out for rain.

They've gone nearly the whole of May without rain and the earth is browning. They've instigated a hosepipe ban in Inishowen, which is something they've only heard tell of in England or maybe Wicklow. All the rivers have run low, and in Glentogher, at the sharp bends under the beech trees, water has disappeared altogether. It's an unprecedented drought. Reserves at Fullerton dam will soon be critical and the long-range weather forecasts are no help. They say the farmers are in danger. That the crops might fail in the fields because there are no irrigation systems.

Cahir is driving to Pollan Bay to sift through what's

blown ashore. He's a bit afraid the gusts will pull weak follicles from their plugs.

Coming down the narrow road that drops in winding turns from the Strand Hotel to the beach, a black jeep is alone in the car park. Cahir comes over the top of the hill, over the fat blown-up daisies, bracing for confrontation. He scans the crescent bay, swinging away broad and gentle for a mile and a half, and he can see the wee fool darting back and forth to the man's feet. Tricked and tricked again. They think they own the beaches, the ones with dogs. They've made the turn having walked the full length to the edge of Cahir's castle. The famous Cahir. Where he plotted his failed siege and hid out his last days before they stuck his head on a pike in Dublin. Graham and Marie have no sense of the pressure of history. To lumber Cahir with the end of Irish Lordship. With the Flight of the Earls and crumbling orders and a failed rebellion.

Cahir kicks the unrooted seaweeds, like slick ligaments torn from missing bones. He skips over a black slug on the path, not squashing him. The usual pickings aren't far away. Ropes, buckets, bottles and caps. Detritus, plastic fragments, spewed by the sea, hawked and retched, thrown with a growl like mucous or pus caught clinging to ribs. All the solid pieces spat from the salty scum. Spitting and spitting and never getting its throat clear.

Cahir's form soured on the drive in from the west, them and their poverty ruining his idea of where he was. How dare they look so rough when Cahir is trying to believe they don't exist? Them and their bare cement, their cracked walls and mounds of gravel piled unhidden inside shitty, rickety fences. Graceless caravans and houses facing each other at all angles, gussied up with asymmetric decking and shiny stone ornament. One-off concrete attempts to keep the grass down and no resources to back it up. A tangle of lawless planning, rusting boilers and skinny donkeys.

He tries to keep his eyes to rocks and water. Little outcrops like Glashedy, like Inishtrahull on the far side of Malin Head, where he'd be reliant on savagery to preserve himself. Perched on a tail barely out of the wash. Where he might be drowned any minute. Nobody has lived on Inishtrahull for decades but the lighthouse beams on, operating by rote in a geography of quietness. The rocks and water and the little port. Deserted, apart.

On the beach Cahir tries to forget men and dogs by walking on the lee side, over a humped slip face, a ridge of stones between him and the sea. A pebble ridge of harmonious grey, peach and coral, rust and slate.

From the height of the ridge, Cahir watches the man and his dog skirt close to the waves, the wee black dog chasing them in and out. When they are slipped by each other, he sits on the stones, listening to the wash and the clatter of tumbling pebbles. The stones are smooth, soft to the touch like they're covered in a fine glittering dust. Alone, at the sea, everything is glittering. The shore is a full world, loud and repeating, shining. He sits until the stones are uncomfortable and then falters upright.

Cahir's bag is full of things he can't save but he picks them up too. The washed orange wrapper of a Coke-can multipack, a white coal bag and an airless balloon. The washed-up dregs of all the things we tried to make. At the remains of a campfire, a circle of blackened stones, he picks up some empty lager cans and a condom wrapper and a red cigarette lighter. The lighter is still working and Cahir puts it in his pocket.

He turns into the wind and back toward the car, his every step like a smash of marbles on the stone hills sweeping around the bay. The shadowed piles of stones eaten into by the sea, shaped into peaks and ridges, like desert sands in the wind.

In the utility room, above the washing machine, Cahir sorts the rubbish into what can be remade and what will have to be buried or sent for incineration. He usually feels better after the beach, the calm that comes with martyrdom, but he can't get comfortable in the sitting room because the fabric of the sofa has gathered Marie's perfume and because the hard structure is poking through the cushions. He has to get calm and there's only one place he can go.

So far, the trees are doing beautifully. They've done so much growing since the spring, full tilt, and the fresh limey green of spring has darkened as they really got to work. It's solid now, a richer, deeper green. So far, the iron water pump hasn't let Cahir down. He's been able to water them every other night or so. He read online that in the first years of growing a tree can be very thirsty and that thirst is much harder to manage for them than hunger. He read that they scream to each other during drought. Vibrations hum in the trunks and they know the meaning. The vessels have nothing to draw and they hum a terrible frequency.

And if they do make it through, they'll never make the same mistake again. They learn and they don't forget. They'll be frugal with water for ever after one serious scare.

Along the hedgerows of the lane everything is dying from the edges inward.

This time, it's a flicker in Cahir to see the cows broken in. To see them in the dry field searching for greenery and moisture, picking in and around his heart for scraps with their obscene tongues. The prickled barrier dried out, thinned and showed its gaps, and it was easy for them to hammer flat. Cahir is too far away to count leaves.

He stands at the top of the field and they hardly notice him behind the piles of dead wood, seasoned and brittled from sitting out. He watches them through the gaps in the pyre, watching them huff and chomp and swing their tails. The field is high with nettles and the purple bells of foxglove. The brambles are in flower and seem to be growing out of the dry husks, the hollowed scrub. It's summer on a hill and it's tradition to make a fire.

Cahir pulls the tangle of dried wood loose. He separates the branches and roots and lays them on the dusty ground, like logs and kindling. He takes the lighter from his pocket. The red butane lighter that was never in the sea, never wet, and the flint system catches and sparks and the flame is immediate. A fire to drive away calamity. A fire to burn up what's harmful.

Cahir scrapes moss from dead trunks and makes a pile from bark and splintered wood. He isn't going to stop.

He picks a torch, a sturdy branch and jams dry tinder in the crook of the tapering twig ends. Cahir blows until there's smoke, blows on the dried-out moss until the fire bursts. The greed of the flame is something else.

He moves once the burning starts. The branch is heavy and Cahir is unbalanced carrying it alight down the hill in the middle of the day. They don't know what he means at first, even with new heat and crackling light in the field. That Cahir is coming to chase them or to teach them, to brand them if they don't run.

The first animal he meets, he holds the fire to her silken glinting hide and she steps away but stops again. He follows her down the slope, near the face of a huge black heifer, yellow and orange light reflected in her wet eyes. He jabs the fire in front of her and when she only turns her back he stabs at her with the torch. She bellows and tears off and he follows her, trying to force her through the gap above the stream. Trying to clear them before the fire burns through heartwood and down to his fingers.

The herd run but don't leave. Cahir comes at them again, too quickly this time, he stumbles on the rocks that rise out of the stream, he trips, losing control and the burning torch is thrown at them. The golden heifer near the bottom of the field kicks and shouts and runs toward the stream, herding her calf too close to the drop and with the fire burning above them, the calf is mad with fright and she trips over the edge and she tumbles into the ditch, on to the rocks and brambles, and she squeals at the cracking noise as she skids, bony legs splayed, banged, broken and on to the rocky bottom of the trickling stream. Howling.

Cahir gets to his feet. His fingers singed. He pulls his torch away from the dehydrated brambles and stands on the kindled ends. He brings it into a clear patch of mud where nothing unintended could light and he sprinkles water from the can on to the smouldering tips, kneeling with his hand held close until the weapon is cool.

The calf is still howling and Cahir can't take the noise. He can't take the baying. The repetition. An alarm. A siren. She won't make it back up the bank. There's no way. She can hardly lift her head. Her leg is lying at an awkward angle, detached.

Cahir keeps the penknife in the wheelbarrow but only for scratching the barks. He only uses it to test for life. On the slight prominence below the woods, they are above the plain and level with the town. Her call will ring out over the valley and Cahir doesn't know how long it would take for her to stop or give up. How long it will take the water to return and cover her. The drought will hold for another week they're saying. She could howl from the dry riverbed for days. He couldn't take it. He wouldn't get away with it.

Cahir climbs down the bank, picking his way carefully over the rocks, through the tangle of nettles and barbs. He crouches low and tries to grab her head, tossing, writhing from the neck. Cahir has to wrestle a hold of her head. She is bony, not fattened, desperate. He gags at the smell of her and at the feel of her coat.

He takes her head in the crook of his elbow, sitting on the ground beside her, and he has to heave at her whole body to get her eyes toward the sky. Cahir looks above him, gagging, trying to see the growth in the old wood, trying to tell himself about mercy. It's kindness to end her pain, he says. He fixes his eye on the hanging branch above the stream. With his free hand and a word about mercy, Cahir slices at her neck. The knife is not very sharp and her hide is tough. It's a rough, deep sawing cut but the noise does stop and the blood does run.

Some Funeral

B irds swarm above the road, blurred in heat that's rising like spray from a rough sea, whipped up by fish in throes. Some of the hedges are holding to white flowers, a summer snow fading dirty and weak, almost ready to scatter and disappear. Dan is recording details for Cahir. So he can pretend he was here in the guard of honour for Susanna Glen, who is dead. Susanna was John's aunt on his dad's side. She worked in the shop for twenty-five years and she's dead at sixty-nine, not overly old. She went downhill very fast over the last year or so. Dementia, apparently. Then a bad pneumonia. Dan heard it all on the slow walk from the house.

All the processions are past them and the chief mourners have taken their places at the pit. The crowds are breaking up and picking heights to get a decent view. Distance doesn't matter because Father McDaid has a microphone to transmit the Rite of Committal. Dan is glued to Lydia and her family, who stand at their own plot a row above the Glens'. Dan knows that they keep it in soil in spite of the extra work that requires. He knows there are flowers in pots and a plaque from Lourdes and a holy water bottle from Fatima. He knows about Francis and Rose and Marianne, all of Lydia's paternal family slipped in beside each other but with no space on the granite to chisel another name. You wouldn't be allowed as many bodies these days, even in a double plot. The cemetery by-laws are too strict.

At the Glens' grave, all the white stones are lifted into animal feed bags and set to one side of where the ground is smashed open and where the hole is vulnerable to fresh air. Where they have dug down to within inches of offensive soil. John was on the final lift and he passes on to Tony and Aaron and the gravediggers who lower the coffin over a pre-laid set of pulleys and straps. Without a word, they heave poor Susanna out over the drop and let her coffin down in small jumpy increments until she is resting on the earth. Dan mutters along with everyone else.

Eternal rest grant unto her oh Lord and let perpetual light shine upon her. May her soul and the souls of all the faithful departed, through the mercy of God, rest in peace. Amen.

Susanna Glen's nieces and nephews cry at the last sight of her. The tears will hardly last but they'll hold her in their general good wishes when they stop and stand at the high cross headstone. Now they stand at the temporary lid dragged over her. The green board that is vivid and spiky like an indoor lawn and set with the family bouquets, blooming outrageously with white roses. A temporary roof heavy with flowers but not strong enough to hold anyone out.

With her choice of plot, Susanna has assured herself a lifetime of visitors at least. Tied herself to those owed more. It'll be a long time before these stones are forgotten, swallowed, fallen or removed. Before neglect wipes them bare of any mark and the reabsorption doesn't matter because nobody wants to find them.

Sweet it were to dwell in fancy out of all pain, says Cahir, and it is amazing to Dan that he can make bland philosophy with his toes sticking out. Dan hates that Cahir's toes are out. It is a hot day but, Jesus, people are trying to eat. People should be able to eat their brownies and carrot cake without looking at Cahir's dirty spags. The wee pink-haired waitress smiles at Dan and he looks after her walking away. Cahir wants to know about the stateliness of the thing.

What? Oh, aye. Very grand, Dan says. Two priests and a Dominican monk. The full choir. Seven altar servers with pious little faces.

A rich woman of the town, buried well with dignified relations in black, nobody distraught. Dan saw them in the shop, giddy as they made the arrangements. Buoyed up with the life they felt in themselves, the faculties required for event management. Hug life close and bark a few orders. All able to walk from the house, all gracious in the hustle and politics of a family funeral. Who will do what prayers? Who will speak after Communion? Dan was there with the other shop workers and is happy to report a lovely service on a fine day. Enormous crowds, with overcoats slung on their elbows. John Glen carrying his aunt's coffin, her body closer to him that it had ever been, cold and closed in. The heights and strides hard to match, the carriers chosen on the hoof. The crowd swollen with payback and parish pump reciprocity.

She was a big Fianna Fáil-er apparently. Devout.

That explains it all, says Cahir. They look out for each other, them ones.

Dan doesn't mention the way Lydia walked beside John, or the way she hugged him outside the chapel door, rubbing his shoulder every time he dropped back from the coffin. Her sad for him, and him happy when she hugged him, closing his eyes and hugging her in to him and his well-cut black suit.

Did you enjoy it? Cahir asks him. It's a great chance to be solemn I always think. O, Jesus! he says, O, Lord! he shouts, Save us from the fires of Hell!

The wee pink-haired waitress is laughing over at them and Dan smiles back at her and sort of shakes his hair out of his eyes. Cahir is gone off mad altogether.

Did you stay for the Glorious Mysteries? Hail Holy Queen and all that. I swear we are lucky to have our wee, whitewashed monarchy, says Cahir. Say what you like about Mary, but she is completely scandal free. Complete and fictional purity. That's what we like. Now Dan, he says, don't dare go burying me in Carn graveyard, I swear. Maybe down at Lagg, he says. Down there you might at least fall into the sea.

New Spuds

Dan has lost any fear of the ice-cream machine. His cone pulling is at a different level these days. Last summer, he pulled some too fat and some too skinny, some too tall and off-set. The drunk peaks hardly propped upright by chocolate flakes, the mess poorly covered by multi-coloured sprinkles and mini marshmallows.

You'd need to start licking, sir.

He thought there would be a rule he could learn or a set motion he could mimic, a gentle swirl of the cone, a quick circle with the wrist, but you just have to stand at the lever and see how it comes. The output varies in speed and consistency so you have to watch and stay calm. It's a skill like anything else. Like kissing or fingering. They all want a poke as soon as the sun is out and it's been mental this last few weeks with the hot spell. All queuing for ice cream to help them understand. To be the man at the cones is a ferocious bit of non-stop work. and you'd be dying for your break away from the cabinet, a brief respite from the barrels and the beaters and asking them is it a milkshake they want? How many scoops?

The first wake on each tub of Gelato is like a fine morning early on, a creamy cold smudge with the look of sunshine. Dan untethers the foil cover and wipes around with his yellow cloth and his bottle of sanitiser, pink as the Tutti Frutti ice cream.

He stands quietly at the till, arranging the Kinder egg pyramid so they face out and are split down the middle; blue for boys and pink for girls. It's a fiddly business but not the worst. The worst is the fizzy drinks. They've no respect for gaps in the impulse minerals department. In the mirror of the fridge Dan is stretched long like he's made of putty, elongated and punched in the nose.

For fuck sake Hugh, you fucking tube, just ram in whatever you can find, is that it? So we don't even know what's missing. Any Mountain Dew? Who knows! The Football Special is in two separate places and has no label in front of either line. But that's grand. We'll all just guess.

Dan sits the chocolate eggs exact, out on the edge so the kids will gurn for them and test for the rare mammy that will let them scream. They scream at each other around the wooden fixings, spotlit and piled with organic cucumbers. The town meeting itself in the queue for a cone or a coffee, or getting sausages for the fry, finding out what the other ones are at. If you're alone with nothing to do then at least you have the limes and strawberries and the new potatoes, just dug.

Sorry, can you get your returns, Christy? They're out the back in the wee basket, Dan says. Like they are every day. But just you leave them there until the fruit loaves are rotting and the flies find them. Life is pitched against us all, Christy. You keep to your defiance and your rotting bracks. A delayed credit note is some kind of victory. That's a good job for you. Ha? Steady. Steady job that. The bread men have it made.

Early to bed and early to rise. Christopher never pissed on his granny's wisdom and, to be fair to him, he's absolutely loaded. The bundle of cash in his front pocket is mental. Christy hasn't bowed to a title. He's riding about in double-denim and Doc Martens, the same rig-out he wore when he was a pirate DJ in the 1980s. You can think what you want about him, look at all that money and smell those rotting loaves. Dan watches him go, the bringer of daily bread, sliding his return tray into the van and the door clipping closed. What's Christy like in the van? In the front seat chewing gum, collapsed to a pinpoint as the hedges and traffic lights flick by. But he's never far away from the next stop and the people prodding him to remind him he's alive. Laughing about United being shite and him promising to get them buns swapped over the next day.

Dan is going to be like Christy. He is plunging in. He is taking up action and he's going to get a big fucking wad of cash. He may as well have it as not. That's what he decided as he cleaned the whipper this morning, initialising the sheet for inspection and counter-inspection. As he drained the sterilising solution from the barrels and poured two bags of sweet, yellow liquid over disinfected steel, his hands clean and sweet-smelling like soap and warm milk.

Lydia still wants to see the world around him. She still asks Dan loads of questions about what he's doing. Where is he? Is Cahir there? What are they talking about? She wants to know who waters the houseplants and who washes the clothes. But there's no more pictures of her bed and no more moaning videos. Just this sliding door. Dan can't understand why she is sending him pictures of a shed door. Pictures and pictures of a corrugated door. Dan thinks the change has something to do with John Glen. In the way she reached out to help him at the funeral and him letting her just briefly, until he remembered where they were. If Lydia wants the distance closed she should have said. She made it seem like Dan had to be slow. Gentle. Like she was recovering from something. Like she wanted to know him first, to trust him. Lydia doesn't think Dan is serious but he'll show her. Lydia might think Dan's going to leave but he won't. He's not going anywhere. He doesn't need anything else. He's going to stay here and they can be together. They can be happy if she gives him a chance. Dan's going to look her in the eye and tell her that.

The Exhibition

And she said, I'll say *nothing* during this holy season of Lent, but when Lent's over I'll *talk*. Dolly gives an outrageous peel, a squealing cackle, delighted with herself for delivering it so well. Do you remember? Do you remember how she used to go on?

Lydia is standing at the cupboard door. The one where they keep biscuits and tinned tomatoes and both white and black pepper. She wants something nice to eat.

Mum? she says, How do you make pancakes again? The last time I made them I was sick.

Do you want pancakes? I'll make a wheen now. Dolly shouts to Sam to see if he wants any pancakes. She gets no answer but starts for the mixing bowl and the eggs.

Lydia edges back from the rising activity. She leans on the edge of the kitchen table looking at Auntie Bee on the wall. Slim and handsome in her nurse's uniform. Lydia does remember how Bee thought and spoke. She would hate what Lydia plans for the garden in Carrick.

Would you not cut the grass dear?

Have you a birdie for me?

Bee was coordinating a visit from a relic of St Catherine when she got the one bad word. On her knees before the candles Father Michael got her. He was very good like that. Father Michael would get you anything for twenty sterling. It was good for Bee she had God then after she had cancer too. Accomplishment behind her, sitting with her feet up, getting tired and thin but still with an important cause to kneel before and a big hall to hold her in state on the night after her death. The silence before the dirge. Carn Chapel provides that at least. A Romanesque monster in hand-chipped granite, it's built for the organ to resound.

. . . I think my days in a gondola are over, says Dolly, but it would be lovely to get a change of scene.

Thanks, Mum. That was lovely. If there's any batter left I'll use it later, OK? I'm away over the fields for a bit. I may do my inspections now. Tell Dad not to bother.

Lydia doesn't have to lie to make her hike. She has official business for her ranging step. Tom is away a few days. A pre-wedding holiday while the cows are at pasture on good dry ground. Her and Sam are keeping an eye on things. Mainly the water trough, that they have enough to drink and that they haven't the growth mown. That they don't need moving on. Lydia has to make a quick count of the herd.

When she finds them in the Well Field above Bee's cottage, she barely stops or wonders at the heifer apart from the group, its head searching for a gap in the whins. Lydia is thinking of Cahir's trees, now with full green hanging on delicate arms, like young dancers, gorgeous in a huddle on the slope.

All of the muck is dried into dust and she thinks she could fill Cahir's watering can at the trough and give the trees a drink. When Lydia comes to the body on the warm rocks, she thinks at first that the calf is sleeping. On its side, head curled in toward its belly. Like they do in the byre soon after they're born. She stands on the bank of the stream and waits for it to stir. Then edges back from the horrible stillness, thinking of a badger or fox. Of fright and separation. Some terror that ran her into the ditch.

Moving away from the steam, she nearly steps on a burnt stick, the black wood flaking, hinting at charcoal. The purification of fire and filters. The leads in her pencils. Lydia bends to examine the dead branch and she wants to carry it home like a relic. Like the bones of the saint Auntie Bee had died waiting to see.

She walks the boundary of the field and in the bottom corner, above the stream, she finds the gap where they tramped through, a new dusty trail over splintered and trampled old trunks and dried out gorse. She comes close to the herd this time and finds the singe marks on their skin. With her phone, she photographs the rough patches, the burnt sections of the hide before going back to the stream to capture the calf in detail. She clambers down the bank and at that distance she finds the cut, the narrow blunt opening and the dried-up blood on the rocks.

At the gate, Lydia searches among Cahir's tools for shears

and secateurs but all the sharp edges are clean. The wheel-barrow is empty and the trowel couldn't have made the wound. Hunkered low, Lydia is close to the watering can and the tinted water. As she tips it, rosy water runs from the spout, splashing on the dry muck and the earth greedily, hungrily absorbs it. At the bottom of the can there is a small knife with a mother-of-pearl handle.

Lydia wants to drag the corpse back to the shed. To hide it and to see it in the room with what it paid for. She would like to hang the slaughtered calf by the hooves from the wooden rafters, hung off a meat hook and a link chain, the meat preserved in brine. Certain foul smells exchanged for others. And surrounded on white boards with all the pretty things that flourish now they're not grazed or trampled. The dried grass heads and foxgloves, the pressed leaves and flowers, the buds opening in time-lapse. Equations and charts, sums on whiteboards that show the ledger. She could drain the little body of blood and smear the white boards, border her flowers and her charcoal figures in a mix of blood and dung and muck. At the centre of it all, her woodblock print in graduated colour.

Lydia will mount the branch on fire and fix Cahir's murder to the wall.

It's all she knows or can think on.

The Show Field

They were hoping for big crowds in the show field. The 104th Inishowen Agricultural Show at Tulnaree was thronged with animals from all over and Dolly was in a state of excitement. Among the organising committee, Dolly had special responsibility for the Home Industries tent and the programme lay open on the kitchen table for weeks in advance. Lydia would read aloud the titles of strange categories and ask Dolly mocking questions about Matinee Jackets.

When Dolly wasn't organising, she was baking. It's in dropped scones and chocolate sponge that Dolly will have to excel if the Carn ICA ladies are ever to wrest the Ceimicí Teoranta Cup from the rival guilds. What with baking and with horticulture, no other countrywoman was entered in as many categories as Dolly. The other women were spread wide. Margaret was focused on the photography and Susan was in for the crochet. Marion and Noreen had put in for vegetables and preserves. Lydia told them it was a wile shame they hadn't bothered to cure any sheepskin. Class 189 had been overlooked completely.

John had said he would meet Lydia outside the Home Industries tent but there was no sign of him when Lydia arrived. She stood for a couple of minutes in the bright sunshine before going inside to see if Dolly had won anything. Lydia walked the long wooden tables, the heat of the tent surprising her as she appraised the entries and the chosen winners. The Overall Category cups and trophies stood on a raised table, shining and polished, ready for new names, or for the same names as every other year. The *McCloskey Perpetual Cup for Best Boiled Cake*. The *Glen Value Shield for Best Butter; two half pound prints, slightly salted.* They were the sort of toss-up that would decide the overall championship. Lydia couldn't see her mum in the tent but at the flower section she found a card that said:

Rose of the Show
Dolly Doherty

Lydia smiled for her. It must have been the hard pruning Dolly gave them last year. She cleared them right to the ground and it is the most perfect bloom. So fresh it should go on for ever. As pure as silk, like apricots in milk. The other categories had no standouts. *Arrangement of Fresh Flowers in a Wine Glass* was poorly supported and the begonias shone luridly in old-fashioned neon. *Wooden Spoons in Wool* is a personal favourite of Lydia's. The spoons made into dolls with painted faces and knitted costumes. Lydia enjoys a weird category, a very specific interest like *Miniature Garden on the Lid of a Biscuit Tin* where everything is home grown and very pretty. Daisies and buttercups and the bobble-headed purple scabius she has in Carrick. She wanted to send Dan a picture of the wooden spoons but remembered that she wasn't doing that any more. Dan wasn't the answer. It wasn't right and she had to stop. She hadn't replied to his last messages.

I'll meet you at the Cattle Show
I'll be in the beer tent in the afternoon
Come out to the show field please. I have something
    to tell you

Outside the tent, Lydia sees John coming with two coffee cups, trying to shake off a man called Drew, the manager in the Bank of Ireland. Lydia watches John and tries to measure what she feels. A fresh test.

I was hoping for a pint, John says, but the bar isn't open so I settled for a coffee. He says she looks great and kisses her on the cheek.

They set off in step, ambling for a lap of the field. Past the striped green and white canvas of the beer tent, erected on the highest part of the field where it will be safe even if the rain comes, its bar built of black wooden boards, the kegs covered as high as the levers. They pass the venison burger bar and the espresso van, a narrow and tense space between them. They give out about the haircuts on the young fellas, like Mikado biscuits John says, and they don't think some of the sheep look right at all.

They're so muscly, Lydia says, like bodybuilders with snooty wee faces.

John thinks the whole scene is silly. Did you see in the food tent there is a prize for heaviest potato?

Lydia tells him not to be sniping about that. It's the heaviest potato Marie-Antoinette has ever grown. John says he never saw a better or a heavier collection of potatoes.

John rang her a few weeks after he came on the floor, after he spattered her inside thigh. He wondered had she any interest in going to the Raft Race down in Malin. The shop had entered a team and really, he felt, honestly, as her boss, that she should come and support the rowers. It was him and Hugh and Mickey and Amanda. They were going to sit in plastic barrels, sawn in half and strung together with a few lengths of rope. There was no guarantee they would float, he said.

Lydia watched them from the bridge, the flotilla cheered off from the slipway, under the birdwatching hut. The bridge was mobbed, black with people spilling out of Lily's and McClean's, hands held out to balance plastic glasses of beer and bags of penny sweets. She kept an eye on the ragged armada as it rowed laboriously toward the Isle of Doagh and the Urris Hills and the sea, as it rounded the little red marker and turned for home. They cheered as the more buoyant crafts came in under the arches of the bridge, a big final push for the podium places. John and the shop team were trailing badly, last place apart from the one team that sunk completely. They went and showered in the GAA clubhouse and came back over to the pub, exhausted, laughing about how Hugh was rowing the wrong way altogether and how the water was up to their knees by the end. It was a very good-natured frenzy of chat and pints. Everybody shouting to be heard.

Lydia was giddy, open, ready to flatter and chide, to be whatever pleased them most. She joked and gestured and held herself as if John was watching and she wanted him to yearn for what he saw. Later, there was music and a call up to sing, and after 'Blue Moon' and 'Moon River' John shouted, Lydia the Master for a song.

The crowd cheered and the pressure couldn't be waved away. Lydia's throat threatened closure, she reached over and took a big drink of John's pint and sat in the corner seat with Marty. She sang an old Julie London song about falling in love. She remembered singing it once in John's garden. The pub went quiet and she didn't look at John as she sang but she felt his eyes from among the crowd.

At the bar afterwards, Kathy McClean from choir gave Lydia a flex of her eyebrows like, good on you, that's some catch for a girl like you.

Lydia asked John about the places he'd been. She gave him a chance to tell his stories about Tel Aviv and Wadi Rum. About Japan and Vietnam and jacuzzi sex in by-the-hour hotels. He answered her old accusations about the family business and she nodded along kindly. It wasn't that easy to stay away, he said. He had to keep it going or wind it up. Of course he dreaded succession planning and all that but sometimes he was glad to have it too. Glad of a duty. To give himself up like that. It's the only way to deserve it, he said. He wanted to build something like his parents had done. He wouldn't abandon his mum and dad.

Lydia told him that when things had gone bad in Belfast, when she wasn't doing that well, she had thought of him a lot.

John is stopped at the *Minute Milking Challenge*. Wait until you see this, he says. I know you don't take me seriously but all my family were farmers too. You won't look at me the same now after you see me working these.

She says that is the risk, yeah.

The girl referee is no more than ten years old but she has a clipboard and John looks to her for direction. He sits at the stool, adjusting himself closer to the plaster of Paris bum of a cartoon Friesian cow, setting his hands on the rubber udders, and at the blast of the girl's whistle he pulls his might. No milk comes at first. He looks at Lydia and at the wee judge in disbelief. There's something wrong, he says. She's bone dry.

He bends over at the teats trying to spot a mechanism, the whole of his arms tugging, pinching and yanking. By the time the milk is squirting the wee girl is blowing her whistle, merciless. She snatches the baker's jug from under the udder and after inspection calls out, two hundred millilitres.

Not so loud, John says to her. I'll not be winning any prizes with that.

John holds the programme out to Lydia, standing close and pulling her in to him. Looking for the competitions he is personally sponsoring. What even is a gelding? he asks.

A castrated horse, Lydia tells him.

See, he says. That's great. I think sometimes that farming is my dream job.

You're one of those?

One of who?

Flowerpot farmers dad calls them.

John said flowerpot farmer was the nicest thing he'd ever been called, except for the time he was named bonniest baby in the late 1990s. I could make a return to the marquee he said, as a former champion. A cautionary tale.

John takes her hand and they walk by the Magic Kingdom Bouncy Towers. Holding hands, wandering around a dry field on a summer's day, past a man with a chainsaw sculpting logs into lions and meerkats, littering round him with off-cuts, sticky with sap. The ice-cream van is out on its own, a big queue at its window, and the goat pens are chock-full and bleating. There are rows and rows of goats, some with huge curling horns, like nightmare toenails.

When John's Aunt Susanna died, Lydia stayed with him for the duration of the wake and the sex was very emotional. After the funeral dinner, they went back to John's house and he said he might love her. But only if she thought that was OK.

This past week, Lydia was euphoric. Manic. Floating with the discovery of a sacrificial death. She started telling John about her work. He was bowled over, he said. Lydia took him into the milkshed because she wanted someone to understand how powerful she was. John was full of questions and Lydia answered them all. About the trees. About Dan and the messages he sends her. About Cahir and the knife and the dead calf.

The horseboxes are open against the boundary wall, their ramps down ready to herd the cargo for home, nettles growing up between them as high as the stone cap on the wall. The bleating of the goats and the glare of their minders prevent Lydia and John from gawking too long, drive them on to the parade ring, where the boys showing cattle are wearing white coats like laboratory technicians.

The judge is Mid-Ulster by the sounds of him, commending the youthful herders as they parade their animals and arrange them in a line. The boys use canes to correct the posture of the animals, to keep them straight and tall and demonstrate the musculature. There is a three-step grandstand to one side for spectators but Lydia and John watch at the fence. She hopes the one with the nose ring gets nothing. There is blood dripping down her nostrils and seeping into the rope where it knots on the metal ring. The wee prick leading her doesn't flinch or worry. He just stands behind her touching her on the shins with his cane to keep her straight. There's a bright future, the man says, for the show in Carndonagh if these boys here stay at it.

They might get us a beer now, says John, smiling, freckles stretched over his cheeks. Will we go and see?

A little girl is squealing on the teacups. Squealing for her mammy every time she circles back around. The mammy is over asking the man who operates the ride can he stop it early. Can they let her off? They'll have no peace until she gets off. They'll have to buy her something now to calm her down. An ice cream or a teddy. They'll have to tell her it's a terrible bad ride and they'll never, never go near it again.

It's a very successful event. Maybe a record year. The crowds are building and it seems to Lydia that they are watched. That she can't get away from performing. Her and John were always at their best in front of a crowd. A sweet couple amplified by one another. Shining harder the more people were near. Teasing the others with the way they touched, with how their shining selves entwined. A crowd to stand around them and clap. To look on jealously and tell Lydia that she's lucky. Special. That she's the best. And they might not even care if it's an honest performance. They might say the technical control was very impressive. At the end, the bow, the verdict, they'll give their ovation, loud and fading quickly.

It was just the two of them in the shed, no audience, and she was wrong to bring him there. Lydia shouldn't have shown him anything. She shouldn't have answered any questions. When John left the shed, Lydia gathered up the pictures, the loose sketches and Polaroids. She tidied them away, filed safe under the sloping lid of her desk, carved with names and symbols. Crying because she couldn't love John after all.

Lydia takes a step to the side so she can face him. So she can deliver another ending. I'm sorry, John, she says. I have to go. I don't think we should do this.

Passing in front of the teacups, momentarily dimming the whirling lights, a farmer in a tweed cap waves at him and John puts on a big smile and waves back. Yes, Frank! he shouts. John waits until Frank is gone from sight and then drops the corners of his mouth. The teacups are swirling round and round and the little girl didn't get off or stop crying. John tries a laugh. An attempt at the beginning of a laugh.

Fucking hell. You're serious?

Lydia looks away and John exhales whatever air was in his nose and throat. I don't get it, he says. The last two months. What the fuck was that about?

I don't know. I wanted it to work this time, she says. I was trying to make it work.

Oh, right. Great. Thanks Lydia. I appreciate you trying so hard. It must be such hard work for you.

John checks himself. He can't be seen shouting at the cattle show. He swells his chest and his hands settle on his hips like when some machine gives up at the shop, like he's trying to figure out the right thing to do, or who to call.

Lydia wants to say that John doesn't love her. That he can't. It's not possible because he doesn't know her. John loves a version of Lydia that hardly exists. A collage of bright pieces she arranged just for him.

It isn't right, she says. I'm sorry, but we shouldn't pretend.

228

The crowds pass around them with ice creams and burgers and the first few are gathering at the beer tent. The animals will be away home soon and then the music will start.

Fuck you, Lydia.

Jesus Christ, what's the matter with you? Can you not tell when something is real? John pulls the end of his nose. He shakes his head. Trying to shake everything away. You're making a mistake, he says. I'm not pretending. This is it. Me and you. This is it.

The words build up and hit. Lydia blinks at the sting.

John smooths the lines of his face with the palms of his hands. I thought you were changed, he says. I'm an idiot. I'm a silly prick.

He is moving away already, his face shifting. She can see him giving her up. Surrendering an idea of Lydia that he has kept alive. An idea that only lives in him. He is leaving it behind, here on this spot and it's something they will both have to do without. I'm sorry, Lydia says again. I really am.

John looks at her a long searching moment. A re-evaluation. Forensic, like he sees all the parts of her now. Sees through the picture she made for him. The parts arranged, coloured, pressed and pressed. Fixed perfect complete. The picture she wanted to be true.

The nearest she has been to a kind of love. It was never near enough. John is moving backwards, away from her, further and further away.

Sorry, he says. Yeah, OK.

*

Lydia is standing still and the crowds whirl around her in their colour and noise. The collected families of the town, crying, laughing, bribing each other. On watch for each other. That they wouldn't lose each other. In one of the big tents, Dolly is giving her demonstration, lit and amplified in a flowery apron. When she's nervous Dolly hums 'Star of the County Down' and Lydia wonders if the audience can hear it. When Dolly was practising in the house, she told Lydia that you have to keep an eye on the cake. That's just the way with a chocolate cake, she said, three or four minutes either side and it'll be ruined. When you're making something, time is everything.

Tom will be back tomorrow and the first thing he'll do is check the herd. He'll want to see every animal. He'll not stop until he finds her, until he sees what damage was done to her. And when he finds the calf at that far edge of the farm Lydia's time will be up because there is a limit to what lies Tom might believe. Lydia will say the trees are hers. A gift for Tom and Ellen to watch from the new house. She'll say and do what she can to save the trees and they might believe a small lie but they'll never believe she slit the calf's throat.

At the top of Bridge Street, walking by Paddy Glackin's, Lydia faces the yellow church and the long white farmhouse, the sweeping green wood. She is stinging all over. Wild with stinging, free, letting everything fall away except the desk in the shed and the work at her hands. The work that needs doing in the shed and at the cottage. The work in the Well Field stretching up to the woods. Everything falling away except the rising voice she can hear just faint.

230

Cahir singing on his knees. His care like a fire under the grey clouds and the steeples of the town, alight on the green floor as he plays with little spikes, bent working in a mad daze of hope. A wrinkle that she noticed and has blown up. An inconsequential rough patch she can't pull away from. She isn't finished.

Sliding the door of the milkshed closed, on her own in the silence, Lydia strains to hear Cahir's tune on the slope. She listens and tries to join in, her own trembling voice in use. She tries to recognise and preserve the sound. Bound up in the song. Belonging to it. Made of it. She sits at her desk and listens for the notes resounding off the cold walls. Just herself in the quiet, at home.

The Two Boys

Dan goes for a poo and his head is spinning. He's muttering as he picks his step over the muck, singing disco lyrics.

In a Portaloo in the corner of the field, Dan has to pop. Intoxicated, like the rest of them. Hammered. A fucking handling banging against his seams. He'll have to settle himself soon, walking away from the lights of the beer tent to the blue plastic box where he's going to chance a shit. Full out of it and a mile away at least from a solid toilet. They all are, the yelping, hooping scuffers doing their best jive steps on the temporary laminate floor. You can jive to anything if you put your mind to it and Dan knows all the basic steps. He has them well practised since Christmas.

Inside, he turns around carefully, trying not to touch anything, tapping his toes on the floor, seeking the piss dribbles that might ruin his suede boots. He puts a cover of toilet roll down over the seat and gathers his silky shirt in around his belly button before sitting. His knees are touching the door but a bit of peace is nice and he can sit on because the boys have done with any understanding of time.

The music is blasting from the tent and the blue plastic door doesn't keep it out.

Dan is thinking about John and Lydia and the cream bun. About the floating dress Lydia wore at the funeral where she was hugging John and rubbing the back of John's neck. Lydia didn't explicitly say she'd meet him, but she will, he thinks, and Dan is going to tell her everything he feels. Everything he knows about her. She maybe hasn't thought through the ways that Dan can make her happy. That he knows how to look after someone like Lydia. Someone a bit different. He knows how to love her. He's going to ask her about the pictures. He's going to ask her to explain. Ask her to tell him what she tells nobody else because Dan really really wants to know. And he might not get it straight away but he has a real capacity for understanding, a real drive toward it. He'll learn enough to help her. They can dedicate themselves to the same ends because Dan knows that whatever Lydia makes will be worth his time. He'll sell for her. Shout for her. Make them all look at what came from her hands. John can't ever love the whole of her like Dan does. If it's money they need, Dan can get money. He's smart. He can make people like him. Dan can get her any money she wants. Big fucking bundles of it like Christy the bread man.

Dan wipes up quickly and jogs over the shitty field,

running and jumping when he gets to the laminate, jumping into the mass of them throwing and thrashing into each other, jumping and shouting, arms in the air like they just don't care.

Rory comes down to them with five tiny glasses filled with something blue. It smells like slushy mix before you add water. The point of it is to make yourself boke early on and then keep drinking. They get a shot of sambuca each and swallow after three.

Are we going or what? Come on to fuck.

In the queue, Mrs Gamble is gatekeeper to the dry-ice kingdom and she nods them in for a tenner, reaping the fruit of her monopoly. At the top bar, it's a throng of foot-ballers and girls in dear dresses but you may stand with whoever's beside you 'cause there's nowhere else to go and they're packed in like sardines. The boys are getting more shots but Dan needs a piss. Strutting, disinterested, fixing his hair, he's happy, doing lines off the toilet seat like he's never-ending.

Dan sees Rory and the boys at the top bar but leaves them to it, heading for the oldies room because he once saw Lydia in there. The lights flash the same and the bar swings in past the double doors, dotted with neon shot glasses and cans of Red Bull, everything sticky with the spillage of relaxed motor systems, overexcited by classic 1980s pop and country standards.

A crowd of young fellas are all eyeing the same girl, spinning, swaying to every hit and beat and for a thing short as a second, Dan goes to take her hand, to start into the sequence of spins and twirls, them jiving, hugging, melting into each other. He's at the edge of the dance floor, going toward her, when 'Rock the Boat' starts and everything shifts. The boys scramble and the girl turns and Dan can see it's not Lydia as she jumps down to the tiles and the tiles light up under her, green and yellow and red, and her skirt rides up a bit, turning blue in the UV and threatening to show how high she did her tan. They don't be long slotting in behind her, legs splayed, stretching their lower backs, swaying side to side, their faces catching with the awkward effort. Sweaty undeniable bodies having a hard time looking cool. There's a photographer lurking, flashing promotional photos, as if they are in their right minds, as if shouting along on the ground, stuck crotch to bum, they are agreeing to the smashed grab, to the mad, unflattering alteration of the record.

In the hall between the coatroom and the toilet, Dan isn't breathing normally. He's losing focus. John was in the beer tent all day and he gave Dan a big hug when he met him in the hall. Conor Clarke stumbles past them, into them, nearly colliding, trying to be polite. Sorry, lad. Sorry, he says, his arms busting out of his shirt, his eyes not squaring.

Do you want a shot? Dan says. Let's get one of those wee blue shots, he says.

John doesn't say anything. He's swaying on the spot. He's holding Dan at the shoulder and he looks a bit serious. Dan thinks it's about the messages with Lydia. The pictures. Maybe John wants to scrap it out. Throw a few slaps in a match-up of strengths and abilities. A contest for the best man to win. Dan tries to shake himself loose and to be ready in his body. He's not going to deny it or lie. He's not done anything wrong. He looks at John's arms and his hands not in fists. He thinks if he punches John, he'll have to quit his job.

Listen, John says, you'd want to have a word with that brother of yours.

Ha? Dan has to shout over the noise from the dance floor.

You'd want to have a word with Cahir. Did you know about these trees?

What? Ha?

John pulls Dan closer to the exit, past the cloakroom and away from the noise. He tries again.

Liddy told me about Cahir and the trees over in Tom's fields. You know how Tom the Master bought your mum's land in Carrick? Well, Cahir mustn't know, cause he's over planting trees. He's over, petting them or whatever. Worshipping them. No, no, wait. Listen. Listen Dan. Liddy doesn't like the thought of him roaming around. So you'll talk to him? She's scared. There's a dead calf, one of their own calves is dead, and she says Cahir killed it. Throat cut like some kind of sacrifice. It's mental. It's fucking mental. You'd need to get him looked at. Honestly.

Dan is smiling at John and making sure his most handsome face is on, flicking his hair out of his eyes, laughing as he shakes John's shoulder.

What the fuck are you on about, John?

John looks him in the eye and waits, like he's very considerate and like he would prefer to spare Dan.

237

Me and Liddy; you know we're back together? Yeah. And you know about the art and all that? That's like them pictures she sold you. She thinks you're great, actually. We both do, lad, seriously. I don't know if she showed you any of the new stuff? But she's serious good. Like, *serious*. And there's this one she's doing now and there's this man in a big coat. On a wee hill, sort of fixing at a tree, and I was like, who's your man? and she said it was Cahir that rents the Good As New.

Dan drops his arm and his handsome face and they're obviously a bunch of fucking fantasists. He wants John to say it again.

John's eyes are closed like he's weary. He's waving his hand at Dan's chest like, calm down, calm down.

No no no. It's right enough, says John. It is. Liddy showed me the pictures of the field and everything. The trees. Wheelbarrow. This wee knife. Everything. She has it all recorded. Just, have a word with him, right? Before the whole town is on to it. Lydia is very serious when it comes to this stuff. She didn't do all that work just to keep it secret. Not that I'll tell anyone. This is just between us, lad, I swear.

Yeah.

Dan doesn't get his coat. He walks outside and straight into a taxi. He doesn't ask the driver anything. Not even if he's busy. He doesn't wait for his change of a fiver. He hammers up the stairs and in Cahir's bedroom door, worrying Cahir's shoulder, standing back for aim.

Cahir spins awake, his eyes searching Dan's face. He lifts his head from the pillow, blinded in the immediate light. Are you OK? he says. What is it, Dan? What's wrong?

Dan is staring around the room. Like he's trying to pick a focus. Like he's afraid to look directly at Cahir. The fingers of Dan's right hand are stretching apart, the tips of his fingers trying to get away from his knuckles. Dan puffs out his cheeks and looks at the ceiling, his back slightly bent as two hands rise to run through his hair, as they run over his face like he's trying to clear something from his skin.

Cahir sits up fully, pulling the covers up under his armpits. Panic is busting through him, wakening him. Fright rouses him very quick. He is looking for signs and clues, at the sweat on Dan's forehead, at the pumping vessels in Dan's neck, at the small movements in Dan's mouth.

Did you cut its fucking throat?

Dan is looking at Cahir to judge the reaction. To learn the truth from Cahir's face and body if not his words. Dan is tapping his nail on the side of the dresser in a quick rhythm unfamiliar to Cahir.

Dan knows about the wee brown calf. In the ditch with its bones snapped. But he won't know that it was an accident or what Cahir was protecting. Or that Cahir is sorry. That the wee thing would have been thrown on a heap once the juicy cuts were butchered. That Cahir was protecting something good and that it belongs to Dan too. He has to tell the truth now. Cahir's mouth is dry. He can't chance too many words.

It wasn't supposed to be there, Cahir says, hearing the fright in his own voice. It was an accident.

Dan had prayed for denial. For anything he could believe. Anger explodes in his belly. He can feel his fingers clenching, grasping around the air for something to wring. He wants to hurt Cahir. He wants to punish him for being so stupid. Him that's supposed to be smart. Dan yanks the covers off Cahir. He grabs the end of the duvet and he pulls until Cahir is bare. His big white body, soft and warm from under the covers. Cahir scrambles and grabs one of his pillows to hold in front of his chest and belly. Dan backs away from the bed.

Wrong, he shouts. Fucking WRONG. WRONG. WRONG. Dan is kicking the base of the dresser and the drawers are rattling, bouncing in their slots. Glass bottles shake toward the ledge and a small money tree in an orange pot falls, fleshy leaves crushed on the carpet.

Cahir takes a long breath in through his nose. He counts his exhale. A calming breath, and when he speaks, he keeps himself low and quiet.

Dan, he says, I think you should go to sleep. I'll explain everything in the morning. I'll show you everything.

It's Tom the Master's land. You fucking idiot. Tom the Master owns all that land. They're laughing at us, Cahir. A big joke for them all. Tom and Lydia and John Glen. Them telling me about you. What about that, ha? So sorry to be telling me everything they know about you. This big joke. Some fat queer slipping about in the muck.

Dan is shaking. A tremor that Cahir can see run through his body, in his fingertips and his upper lip.

I'm going to take them out, Dan says. Show me where they are and I'll take them out. Now, Dan says, like it means the last chance.

Cahir gets up and grabs his dressing gown from the bedpost. He moves toward Dan pulling on his robe. He doesn't recognise Dan at all. He wants to calm him. Soothe him. He'd say anything to make Dan sound normal.

Dan, he says, I did plant some trees but that's not right about it being Tom the Master's. It's Mum's land. Ours. You and me. I know you're upset, Cahir says, I know you are, but they're not right and they shouldn't have told you that.

The steady pacing of Cahir's pleading, his attempt at explanation, seems to Dan so full of spite. How dare he be this weak? So pathetic underneath him. Dan stops pacing, stops tapping and kicking. He fixes up his shirt and trails his finger under his nose.

No, he says. You don't know. You're just a waster. You don't know anything about me.

Skipping the stairs and banging the back door so that Cahir knows he's gone, Dan is sprinting down Molly's Brae, past Porters' and Dr Friel's. The road is quiet and the night is still and the quick clap of his boots on the footpath is the only noise. The hill is steep and each bound shudders into his knees as he runs through Churchtown, past Moore's and the Hokes' and into the Masters' yard with the big alder tree and the long milking parlours and Dan is at their door, the cottage door in the oldest part of the house, before he can get breath into his lungs, or feel the cold, or before his chest shrinks back. He wants Lydia to know how it happened. If he doesn't correct her now, everything will be wrong for ever. If Lydia comes out, he'll tell her anything she wants. He'll tell her all the things he meant to earlier. He'll cry or swear anything. There's nothing he would keep from her if she comes out wrapped and cold into the middle-night light. Bang on the black cast composite door, they'll

lift their heads from their pillows, they'll wonder at the
noise of a knock, pat around for slippers and dressing robes.
Dan will make a new future for them. He rubs his face
roughly, digging his fingers into his cheeks and rearranging
all the skin on his forehead. He can't stop. He can't let
them. The fuckers. They think they have him now. They
think they have him beat.

It's not full darkness. An old orange light glows over a
scabby tomcat, bounding lithe across the yard in panic. Dan
watches him skip the concrete and dash into the true dark
of the hayshed. The sheds are low and of mixed materials,
not built at once. They run perpendicular to the house and
away from it, toward the cow byre and the dark. Dan knows
the door under the soft light. The blue corrugated metal is
very familiar to Dan because he has seen a hundred pictures
of it. It's as familiar to him as something he owns himself.
There are no lights roused in the house. Nothing to make
him turn and sprint. His blood is up, pulsing so quick it
makes a mess of a minute. The door is locked but the key
is tucked under a crumbling breeze block.

Dan slides the door closed and stands in the darkness.
The light from the yard seeps in the edges of the door and
through the window, collecting in the corner of the room.
It's gradually enough to see a long series of pictures stuck
up with Sellotape. Pictures from a distance, of a blue overcoat. The specific crouch of the man in the coat stabs
through Dan. He pulls them off the wall and moves into
the light at the window to see them up close. The dead calf,
its broken leg and blood-shot eye, the tear across its neck.
Cahir at his desk in the shop, shot from across the room,

from the green velvet chair. Dan sent her that picture. He can't think. He can't understand. He can't believe someone would do this to him. That he could be a toy for her. A teasing game. Deep gasping breaths rake through Dan's chest, covered lightly in his stupid silk shirt.

On a table in the middle of the room there is chunk of wood, gouged and chipped, painted with vibrant colours. A stylised image of the man at work. A version of it, not exact. A representation of the green woods, of the town in grey, with steeples rising like smoke from all the chimneys, the man in blue kneeling on the gentle brown slope that slips down to the stream. It looks to Dan like an old poster, or postcard.

Around him there are paint pots and pencils, paper and copper. Copper plates etched with single trees. There are hundreds of Polaroids and sketches, printouts of all the stems, close up in all weathers. A wheelbarrow. A shovel handle poking through the hedge. Trowels and forks and shears. A trampled fence made of old branches. It's a shrine. That's what it is, and Dan can tear it into as many pieces as he wants. Her sleeping and everything torn to pieces. The evidence erased. Dan wishes he could piss over the collected artefacts, leave some stain on the record, like the boys who threw eggs at the High Cross and left dribbles down the ribbon of the East Face.

He can't stay still. He's itching. He's so hot. His skin is crawling with heat and the itch is going to eat him up unless he gets moving. He throws the wooden block at the corrugated door and runs. Through the yard and out the gate, wandering in aimless figures at the meeting of the roads.

Dan climbs the gate of the field opposite the house, his legs straddling the galvanised rungs. Hinged off concrete posts in a boundary of sweeping, tensile wire. It's all Lydia's and right under her gaze. He is under her window where he stands. Her sleeping even though it isn't fully dark and he won't sit because, Fuck. Fuck them all. Fuck her and her spoilt narrow sadness. Let her smother in it.

Dan jumps down and darts through some of the swathes in her possession. All in black with his feet skimming over the grass and wetted by the dew, he runs in as far as the telephone pole, drunk in the middle of the field and slick with what looks like black candle wax, like tar that's warmed up and dripping. His every quick step makes a small noise on the short grass, recently cut and saved, raw and yellow with only a ring of lush growth at the edges where the blades were steered clear. He tried to correct the record and that's all he can do. She doesn't want his help or care about being right and good fucking luck to her.

His phone is buzzing but he lets it ring out and ring out again. He can't go home. Not back to hiding.

He drops his phone in a water trough at the gate and walks on. It has to stop. This way of living that's pathetic, that's laughable. That's just like death, lying back and inviting them in. A husk to be broken apart with hedge clippers and handsaws, ribs yanked open by the full weight of living bodies, crawled over in desperation at the resistance of a ribcage. It's urgent that Dan protect the cavity. It's urgent that he preserves a heart.

Dan walks back to the town where there's always an open house for ones who can't let it stop. Who can't stomach themselves just yet. Dan doesn't know any of the boys there but nobody cares. He has some money left and they have pills that he can take. He can see them swimming, laughing, egging him on. Dan feels sick and horrible but the pumping inside him won't stop. It's driving on and on and it won't stop until he has it finished. Until he's done something bad. It's too late anyway. What he said is too much already. It's the worst thing he's ever done because Cahir has nobody. Nobody at all except Dan and Dan knew that even as he was taunting him. And now it's done. And all that life of innocence and care and of one watching for the other, it has to be over. Dan can't stay with Cahir now because they can never have again what they had before. Cahir that loves him. That can't forgive anything or ever forget it.

The Flood

The rain stopped but Dan didn't come home.

The thunder continued for hours without lessening and the rain fell straight in heavy drops that were close to each other, almost continuous streams. The power cut after Dan left and Cahir went back to his bed. He tried to sleep, listening to the thump of the rain and the thunder overhead stirring him. It kept going, fed inexhaustibly. A loop that seemed eternal. Cahir got up when he saw the bathroom light come on, once the power came back. There was water pooling on the lawn and on the radio they said that all the bridges were washed away. Twenty-three bridges on the peninsula washed away. Cahir didn't know they had so many bridges or that their home was really an island. That there is risk in having so few routes out, passing through a slight land bridge, a low and narrow isthmus, recovered only when waters fell. They walked across borderland and they made their settlements with no thought for old names and now one exit is impassable and the other is considered perilous. It is impossible to reach Buncrana, they say. They are sending the army, to build Bailey bridges over the gaps, they are setting up lights and controls and one-way systems over the hills, so that they can drive slowly over the pre-fabricated trusses and pretend normality can be reclaimed in time.

The water of three wet days came down in two hours and the soil was saturated long before it stopped. The rivers burst and ran in old forgotten courses, clearing away foundations they didn't know they needed. Cars were torn along and smashed through kitchen windows. There was a mudslide in Urris and the waterfall in Clonmany did real damage. Whole flocks of sheep and herds of cattle were destroyed. A flash flood in a sodden place is a betrayal because they are well used to water, the rain is constant and familiar, but not like this. Not with watermarks up to the lintels and great holes torn from below the roads in Iskaheen.

Cahir walked all over the town looking for Dan. Every road he knows. He is still walking.

He doesn't know what else to do. Where else to go. He left a note on the table and so many messages on Dan's phone. It can't be true. Why would it be true? That he would be so wrong about everything. Cahir has had visions of the water all morning, the torrents risen from the ditch and the rudderless velocity uprooting everything. Floating bones and rotten hides and currents ripping open the soil. Cahir staggers over the lane past the sign for the Mass Rock with his hood up, sheltering under the full canopy. His head won't settle. He can't get it to settle. He has to know what's true.

The water is gushing in all the gullies. That's what he can hear in the hollow. The water is hopping, gagging, throttling through the channels. Cahir is on the bank above the stream and there is no sign of the wee calf. The water is too high. He doesn't want any secrets. If Dan will just come back, Cahir will confess everything. Lay his sins in the open. He climbs down, trying to stamp on the brambles and the nettles but they bend and evade his shoes and they sting and pierce him and he climbs on down and now, even close to the water, there is no sign of the calf and he doesn't want her to be washed away. Cahir doesn't want the evidence to be flushed because he doesn't deserve to be let off with killing her. He did it. He ruined it like he ruins everything. Like he ruined himself and Dan too.

Cahir steps into the violence of the water whispering his only prayer. He can't stay upright. As soon as he is off the bank, the torrent whips his feet from under him and he's tossed into the rapid flow and thrown against the rocks.

The water rushes at his eyes and into his mouth. He is choking, drowning. The swollen water flips him and throws him and tears him along the stony bottom of the bed. When his feet hit the bottom he kicks into the earth and drags himself on to the bank. He's spluttering, coughing up water, pulling himself up into the brambles. He tries to pull himself up but the tangle of shoots isn't strongly rooted and the thorns are large and sharp. Cahir calls out in pain at the breaking of his skin. He pulls himself to his knees and crawls out onto the flat earth. He lies on the grass gasping, retching.

Cahir has no right to have anything spared and he can hardly look at them. He falls to his knees. Praying in the muck and the rain for Dan. The earth is soaked, turning liquid. It coats Cahir's hands easily. He rubs it into his hair, matting it down, banging at his head and scraping his scalp. He can feel the hairs coming loose and sticking to his palms. He brings the crown of his head to the ground, into the wet muck and he grinds his head down into the earth. He wants to dig himself into it. He wants to fucking drown. Eat the fucking muck. Fat fucking queer. Joke, fucking waster. He wants to eat the earth until he pukes his guts up. Until all he's puking is the dirt.

He wishes he'd never done any of it.

Nobody knows where Dan is. Cahir rang Oisín and Rory and even the shop. He cringes to remember the calls. Asking them to help. Telling them something might be wrong. Them knowing that Dan must hate him. Them knowing it's all Cahir's fault. He texted Dan to tell him.

i'm sorry, he said

please

please send me something. anything. anything please

Dan would never not reply. No matter what, he would reply. Something bad must have happened. And if Dan is hurt, or worse, it's Cahir's fault. He wasn't his right self and it was such a bad night. A once in two hundred year event. A great flood. Cahir saw a video of a man wading through the river at Simpson's and the guards said it was a miracle no serious injuries had been reported. How long will Cahir wait to tell them? His knees are bouncing on the earth. He is rocking on the spot. His fingers are gripping his temple and he is shaking. He is screaming into his gullet, mouth closed, hoping something might burst. That some other dam might be flattened, some inner river might overflow and end it. Cahir reaches out for a stone from the banks of the stream. He puts his left hand flat on the wet ground and raises his right. He hammers down at the tips of his fingers, smashing again and again until the new pain is all he can feel.

A Small Ruin

Dan woke on a stinking sofa. Him and Jamie Smyth together in a scabby living room. Dan didn't feel good. He was sick. Still not right. He wanted out of the room and to believe there was light on the other side of the blocked-up windows. Dan sat up and the sofa springs creaked. Jamie stirred in the armchair, but resettled himself, rubbing his thick nose. Dan walked to the door, the floor creaking too and the door handle was clangy and echoed into the empty space. Jamie was wakened. His eyes came at Dan through a haze and Dan wanted away from them and what they knew. From whatever way they had been rearranged.

Dan stepped outside the room, outside the house, and heaven was open, emptying itself. Water was tipping down, bouncing on the footpath. The noise shook through Dan, a rough growl, the middle and echoed outskirts of thunder.

The sky flashed alight and the growl answered and the rain fell straight on to the streets, rivers pouring from the sky, the sky captured all the way to two different seas. Dan hadn't even a coat.

He clung to the doorways on Pound Street, Styrofoam and tinfoil trays floating in from the chip van. He stepped under the arch that joins the Park bar to the bookmaker's, a covered lane as far as the car park of the supermarket. He ran for it.

The key for the forecourt cabin is on a hook inside the heavy grey door, beside the alarm panel and keypad. Dan took the key and ran from the door to the shelter of the forecourt canopy. The drops beat on the roof and on the cabin with a mechanical roughness. A dangerous, quick slop of a noise. Dan got inside the cabin quickly and found Michael's yellow, high-vis jacket. The one he wears on the most violent days. He shuddered at the warmth and the dirt of it, reflective bands streaked with sludge. Michael is a really decent lad.

Dan left the key in the cabin door and roamed the hidden edge of the forecourt. He stood at the kerb where water and petrol don't mix as they run into the drain. Pooling rainbows washed away by what's pumped from the tanks and what leaks to the margins. It was an hour or two at most, his rest, and it wasn't enough to cut the circuit. While he was standing there, two beams of light swung in the car park gate and approached him. Dan was glowing in his coat. Everything wearing off. Everything falling into flat revulsion. Him remembering himself and the things he's done. The window of the driver's seat began to drop and Dan stood still, waiting dead-faced for them to go on show. Steeling himself for whatever excuse they were claiming today. How they were going to excuse themselves for being a reflection, for holding so desperately to their frame.

Are yous open? the man said. He didn't get an answer but that didn't stop him. Would you put me in forty diesel?

There was an ulcer on the tip of Dan's tongue, just sprung up and he hooked his tongue in around the ragged spike of his lower canine, slipping the stinging tip in around the jags to clear the ache in his temples. Ulcers are a sign of being run down.

Are you OK yourself? the man asked.

Dan pulled no expression of cover-up. For the first time in his shop-life, he didn't try and please an opposing face. He started to walk off. He was finished with that place. With the dopes chugging about, their bodies humming, their cheeks aglow, opening their mouths with feeling, or pretend, to ask about the raspberry and amaretto chocolate slice. How it's only another euro with a large latte.

Dan is not as weak as that. He's not afraid of being shown up or of looking John straight in the eye because he's not any worse than John Glen. Not any less. Dan has no sore spots, no deference toward these dickheads and their well-kept graves. He has no need to be in fiddling with honeycomb wrappers, so slippy they fall into the Dairy Milk bars. Thanks be to God Dan hasn't many bones sunk on the Barrack Hill, none he really knew or cared about, because there is nothing as good as bones for tethering. The granite headstones streaked with birdshit anchor them to a certain hillside. Lydia and John and people like them, they haven't a line dropped anywhere else. They can't move too far from their small hereditary thrones. They'll never know how they would fare without soothing names, far from the places they own. Dan was free as long as he could hold apart, nothing to keep him from walking into the heavy rain, pulling his diesel-smudged hood up over his ears.

He is still walking, pounding up the fields, flushing it out, sure now that there's no way to bring the parts back together. At the top of the first field, the barbs on the fence catch his crotch as he swings his leg over, trying to use the wire rungs like a stirrup. Unused to how they sink with his weight, they knick a hole in his trousers. Dan's good work trousers with a new gap for rushes to stick in and prickle him.

Dan follows the hard paths as long as he can, until there's only heather sweeping on the hill and then he jumps from clump to clump in big strides, guessing after support and jolting drops. He sometimes chooses only an offshoot, froth that doesn't hold him, and in the moment of falling he's already hiking back up with thighs and hands grasping. He tears the grasses as he goes, twirling them in his fingers, creasing them and twisting them until they lose their freshness and his legs are wet up to the new hole in his crotch and covered in grass seeds. He's sweating in the rain. The rain that must stop soon, unless the whole world is to be underwater. The rain that must pass now the thunder is gone. Dan wanted the world to wake him up but he didn't imagine how heavy the water would be. He wades the streams, not even looking for a bridge he's so wet, the water a lurid orange like Irn-Bru.

He's not recovering. Not a dab hand. There's a sharp stick drumming at a taut kind of thinning skin. The sharp end is angling in and now it's started he can't make it stop. Dan will have to leave now because waiting around isn't working and no matter how long and hard Dan studies, he'll not settle as native. He did find their script very funny. He thought it was a charming store of lines to choose from. Dan thought he was lucky. That by chance he had found something that couldn't be bought in the world. Right at his nose, something basic and rare. But nothing is as sweet or pure or as good as Dan thought. The house lights are full and harsh and they make the stage look so stupid and small and Dan can see how ugly the actors are. The ones who never made it or never left to try. Gurning in heavy make-up that stops at their jaws. Shrieking in cheap re-purposed costumes. Their set battered, scuffed, smelling of sweat and hairspray and cigarette smoke. Them thinking they were excellent or even capable when the smell of failure is everywhere and only more noticeable as you get the odd gasp of air. The whole space filling with a stench, a sweet sneer that's rotten like a bad pear turning black and mulching apart, catching on your clothes and under your nails. And listen, it's fine. Dan can't cast off life. He hasn't even tried it. He closes his eyes against the feeling in his chest. The wriggles that have taken root in the caps of his lungs, threatening to smother him, to prevent easy exchange of air. Dan is relieved to remember the anatomical structures. They're what will help him escape.

When Mags left the deli to work in a crèche, because that's what she studied for and it would be a shame not to use her degree, they gave her flowers and a card and a handbag out of River Island with leopard print on it. There were real tears but Mags couldn't stay because it would never be good enough for a girl with an honours degree. Dan thought she was a dum-dum. A dose. And now look at him. Ta-da marketplace of futures! What reward for the handsome and clever? Just as dumb as Mags, looking to climb out of his box. Boring and obvious, falling in with their silly myths of personal achievement, but what else can he do? Honestly. If anyone knows, go on and tell him. Because what if his face settles ugly? When his hands are mangled from hauling crates and threading cages through doors that are barely big enough for them. What if he's at his physical peak and he never has anything else to lord over John Glen? Stuck. Bowled over. Dependent on annual bonuses for his mortgage. And once he has his own wains to rear, life spinning by in a blip of toenail fungus and lower back pain and every wee victory swallowed in one big summary. He can't piss his time away. He has to stop miniaturising himself just to make things easy for Oisín and Rory, or John and Lydia, or Cahir.

The rain has finally stopped and Dan is soaked to his skin. His feet are squelching by the time the heather falls away and he finds another path, worn by sheep among the whins and this is the path that takes you to the ruin where they said a monster lived. A fairy king or a wizard. Cahir was very good with magic and stories. Meticulous, he never skipped to the end, and he always made a big effort with the voices. He read on and on and he never said no or that's enough. Dan was waiting for the stories to stop but they never did.

The two of them would come up this hill in summer and Cahir would explain where everything was. How their world was orientated: the compass points, the geography of towns and seas, the history of settlement on the plain. Dan pinches the bridge of his nose, afraid to let go in case he dissolves in the heavy air.

Cahir is trying so hard to ignore it all. A subversion so small and shabby that everybody leaves him to it. Cahir and the horrible shapes he pulls trying to stay hidden. It's the compensation of a body in pain but Dan can't stay to give him cover. It's not his job to protect or shield or fix Cahir. That wouldn't be expected. He can't live a certain life because Cahir made some bad choices.

Way above the town, an eaten gable of tan stone topples on a natural brow above the woods, and three old hawthorn trees have grown wide in the time it took the walls to fall. There are flies swarming after the rain and there are purple flowers on the thistles. The feathery purple heads are up to his shoulders and he is completely wet. The town is below him: woods, chimneys and rooftops, the flat ground that runs from Culdaff to Churchtown.

Dan flattens a path through the nettles keeping his hands held high. He has to touch the wall of the old house now he's so close. You couldn't come this far and not put your hand on the moss. At the back of the house where they would have felt the sun on a good afternoon, Dan climbs up on one of the walls, stepping gingerly from block to block, testing them for wobbles and the dissolution of old mortar. The dragonflies are following him. A cloud of them stifling reverie. He tracks back on the same path, only willing to forge one line in the grass.

Dan tries his usual route home but the fields that lead to Moore's gate are flooded. A new brown river is flowing diagonally across the hill. It's moving too fast to chance and Dan is pushed a little further north. He heads toward the houses at Woodtop and if he can't find the way out there, he'll have to track back and search for the Mountain Road. There are more and more trees around him now, not just the odd pioneer in the heather.

Cahir didn't know and it's only a small crime. Asking for the facts would sound to Cahir like asking for help and he couldn't have telegraphed his care like that. He couldn't even ask Dan and that's a shame. If he could have asked Dan for help, everything would have been OK. Dan will say sorry even if that will admit last night into fact and Cahir will forgive him. He has to. Dan's nearly back to himself. They can do this with kindness. It's not a tragedy to live in the way that is common. He has an easy way out and Cahir will be all for it. He'll say that Cahir should come too. To London. Or apply now and head over next year. Really, the two of them together would be a serious outfit. There's nothing they couldn't do.

The woods are beautiful once you're in the middle of them. In all his time in Carn, Dan never heard anyone mention them but they're lovely. That's probably what carried Cahir away. Thinking he was the only one to notice something.

Dan can see rooftops through the trees. He can see the

dome and steeple of the church and the red square of the supermarket. He can see the hills behind the town on the way to Moville. He can see smoke rising from chimneys and he can hear the road a little clearer. He can hear that the road is very wet. He can hear the birds and smell the damp of the soaked floor before the trees start thinning, coming to an end at a ditch of coursing water, a clearing and a short slope of nettles and dock leaves and very small trees.

Dan closes his eyes because it's very hard to have your heart break and keep looking at the world. Because Dan's world is getting worse, right in front of him, and he can't bear to see it narrow, to watch it turn and corrupt. A scruffy bit of ground on the outskirts of the town. Dan doesn't know it. The physical dimensions of the place are new to him. He's been living in the shadow of a place he didn't know existed. But it's the figure of the man Dan is looking at. When he opens his eyes again. In fear. In disgust. It's Cahir he is looking at. Not the components of the earth.

Cahir has been in the water too. He's soaked. His hair is plastered to his head. His face is covered in muck and blood. He is shouting to himself, swinging a spade in his right hand. His left hand is held close to his body, cradled in at his belly. In a field of small trees, shouting. Unheard. Dan can't hear the words because the rushing of the water in its stone channels is deafening. The water is running down the slope, too quick for roots or soil to absorb. Running over the earth like it's concrete or tar, desperate to find a drain or gully, some channel that will take the force of it and run underground or to the sea.

Cahir is pacing in a big circle with the spade in his hand. He drops the spade and raises a hand to his forehead, like he's trying to keep out the light, like he might see better in the shade. Searching, peering, unseeing; his lips are moving. He's spitting at himself. His lips are moving violently. His chin is banging down and out, making big shapes, like he has no room for the words he has to say. His whole head is led and strained by the run of words pouring from his mouth, like Cahir is the source of the flood. A man possessed, turning on the spot, gesturing in the air with the one hand, his body in a fit of begging, a thrashing stream spat, pained, into the air with as much force as the world around him. A fit of tongues from a desperate mouth. Incomprehensible in the other noise. Animated with something terrible, something that could be profane or divine but which is incomprehensible to the unbeliever. Dan is not wrecked by the same spirit. He doesn't understand. He can hear the spill of speech-like noises carrying through the throttle but communication is impossible. Consonants and vowels burst out in varying pitch and volume, speed and intensity. Cahir fully yielded to prophetic terror. To utterances not known in any other place on earth.

Dan watches him drop to his knees and tear at his hair. Silent. He looks at his palm, like it's responsible for a crime. His one good hand grabs at his stomach, then his chest, clawing, he tries to pull himself apart. He bares his teeth and tries another roar. He rises with the building pressure and lurches at the little stalk next to him. He pulls it out and drops it at his feet, like it's burning. He stamps on it and the snap is lost in the throttling water. Cahir moves on, quickly now, small steps over the muck as if he's going to pull the others too. As if he'll get it done now it's started. Like he's afraid to stop.

It was Dan that ordered the uprooting and though he longs to back away and hide, he can't watch Cahir undo himself.

Stop, Dan says.

Too quiet. Muffled. Drowned by the moving water. It was too small a sound to make a difference. Dan tries clearing his throat. He tries to engage the mechanisms. The physical reflexes which would give him voice. He steps into the open and shouts his brother's name above the slushing roar.

Cahir scrambles at the noise. Looking around like mad. Unable to tell any meaning other than threat. His coat is wet and heavy and it hangs and swings around him. He searches the boundaries. He picks up his spade and crouches low, moving to the gate. He is trying to hide.

Dan shouts Cahir's name again. He is standing on the bank opposite Cahir now, waving, bright in his high-vis jacket, his throat clear, calling loud for Cahir to stop. To wait.

Dan climbs down the bank a bit and launches himself to the other side, on to the nettles and brambles. He stamps on them, trying to keep them under him, trying to crush them under his feet as he comes up the other side. His hands grabbing so he doesn't fall back, picking up new stings and bruises. Dan steadies himself, picks himself upright, his toes and shins and knees battered on the stones. He walks up the small slope toward Cahir. Frozen still, Dan can look into Cahir's face because Cahir is looking at the ground. Staring at the little thing under him that he destroyed. Dan comes right up close. There is fresh red runny blood at Cahir's temple and streaming from his lip. His left hand, held across his middle, is bleeding and swelling. The pulps of his fingers are bust. Dan gets on his knees and picks up the tree. He is looking for the hole so he can put it back. He scans the earth for the planting spot so that he can look away from Cahir's hand.

Why didn't you answer me?

Dan stays on his knees, holding the broken tree. He tries to set it in the ground, into the small hole that is black at the bottom. The roots are a good tangle, a mass of tendrils, thick and thin, they sit back happily and Dan firms the soil over them but the tree doesn't stand again. It's broken below any of the branches. Finished.

I lost my phone, he says.

Cahir is nodding. Like that makes sense. Like that was understandable.

Dan stands up and smiles. Here, he says, come here. You're soaked. Dan's voice is soft and tender. Stripped of every hardness and defence. Cahir, he asks, what did you do to your hand?

Dan reaches out for Cahir but Cahir pulls away, sharp. A snapped jolt, like the touch was a shock. Like he'd had a frightening pain shoot through him. His whole body jerks and he opens his mouth. The skin around his eyes scrunching. His right hand goes up to cover his ear, like the noise of the water is unbearable, and Cahir starts to cry.

I didn't mean to embarrass you, he says. It was Mum's land, he says. It was ours, I promise.

Cahir's face is a bloody scrunched up mess and Dan

doesn't know how to help. He tries to get near Cahir again. Tries to touch him, moving toward him, opening his arms. Cahir lifts his head and opens his eyes. He lets Dan close and Dan takes him. Dan almost jumps the final distance and he hugs Cahir very close. He rests his hand on the back of Cahir's neck and he squeezes very tight. He hopes Cahir can feel it. Dan will try every trick he knows. He'll pretend anything. Do whatever it takes to keep Cahir together. Live any life to mind him.

Cahir detaches himself and stands a little back, looking away from the trees and toward the town. He wipes his mouth and swallows as if it's over or as if it's only a mess and he'll clean himself. As if he's fine now except for the blood on his hands.

Let's go, Dan says. Come on now.

Dan leads Cahir from the place unseen because they shouldn't be there. He gives Cahir his yellow, reflective coat and pulls up the hood, wiping some of the muck from Cahir's face and hair. He can feel the space closing. The space that was big enough for him too. Cahir was split on the table, open for repair when Dan found him but already the space is closing. He can sense Cahir withdraw and he's almost relieved to see it. He can see Cahir pulling together on the walk home, not a spare word for Dan. Not even a whisper. There isn't a twitch in his face. His mouth is set, clamped shut and so is any chance that Dan had to know Cahir or to live again the lives they dreamed of in the past.

Penny Baps

Four months later

Two blond children roll around on the window seat between exotic pot plants. Cahir knows the children to see. He has been a disciple since their dad turned up to brew at Banba's Crown, a parked-up shrine to the Celtic goddess of small-batch, hand-roasted coffee. A rickety food cart ready to meet you on the walk back from Hell's Hole. Out front, the same poppy-red shines under a gloss coat, a bloody entrance to a wooden fairy fort, and Cahir hides inside under disco balls and the cover of the glossy espresso machine, huge and curving white. The kids are making a racket as they scramble for the door after their mum. It's a cheerful sound as it recedes. Cahir sits at the bench over the window seat and twirls the fronds at his fingers.

The girl with the pink hair comes delivering coffee. A red mug on a red saucer and a small jug for milk.

Thank you, he says in a funny voice. That sort of weirdo voice is why Cahir has to live above The Spice Palace. He has taken the flat because it's only forty a week and he can't keep living on Molly's Brae, not now that Graham and Marie are back. He painted it white and put down a blue carpet. He dismantled the fish tank and the broken oven but there were no parts good enough to save. It might suit him to be in the middle of the town as long as he doesn't get fat on naan bread.

For weeks Dan was saying he wasn't going. No way. And nobody was going to make him. It was Cahir's chance to keep his days intact. By saying nothing, or with just a hint of weakness, Dan would stay.

Cahir is lucky to know the appearance of repair. How to make a thing look solid and usable, like it's fit for its purpose. It was great preparation, all that strong glue and sticky tape. He learned to spot the giveaway signs of damage and how to soften and brighten them. Often you can rub the rough spots smooth, but sometimes it's better to cut them off. If you don't have much time, excision is sometimes the answer.

Cahir didn't have a lot of time to make Dan forget blood dripping on the muck. He only had a few weeks until their chance was missed and he knew that Dan wouldn't buy any false strain. Not jokes or declarations. Only solidity would ring true.

They never mentioned the tears in the clearing or the

row in Cahir's room. They never apologised for the ways that they were right or wrong. They cut away the memory of it. They went for coffee and sat through films and Cahir gave out about explosions. They drove to Leenan fort and explored all the underground passages. They hiked the back fields to the ruined house and said goodbye to monsters and kings, to the rippling hills and mounds where they had lived their whole lives and run out of things to find.

Cahir started talking about the future, and in the future, Dan doesn't live at home. It's one small and simple change. They have a different way of going on in the future. In the future, they aren't together in any one place but they still tell each other the best new things they learn.

Eugene the window cleaner is under Cahir's nose, blocking his view across the road to his new lodgings. Eugene lets down his bucket, rests his wooden stepladder at the wall and sticks his head in the swing door to ask permission. The girl with the pink hair looks up and shouts to him before he has the door fully opened,

Yes, Eugene! Aye no bother, just you work away.

Eugene has everything he needs outside. There is steam wafting off his bucket and Cahir wonders where he keeps the kettle. Right under Cahir's window seat, Eugene squirts Fairy Liquid into the bucket and mixes it with his finger until the suds rise. It's a fine bucket, split in two halves. One for suds and the other for rinsing water. Cahir watches him move back up the street, to the top window beside Pat Kelly's and work his way through the hooks on his belt. A soapy rag first to lift the dirt and smears, the more obvious articles, soaking the surface and letting the suds run.

You couldn't say it isn't useful to wash the windows. They are sparkling across the street in Bridie Fintan's. Soon, he's at Cahir's window, a sudded sponge on a stick and then a squidgy blade dipped in clear water, leaving sharp edges squeaking after him.

There was a notice in the paper.

I, Tomas Doherty, intend to apply for permission for development at Churchland Quarters, Carrick, Carndonagh. This development will consist of a single storey dwelling house, domestic garage and all ancillary services including connection to main sewage and water lines.

A copy of this application may be inspected or purchased at a fee not exceeding the reasonable cost of making a copy, at the offices of the planning authority, during its opening hours.

Marie gave Dan the whole story. How Tom the Master had approached them way back. How he was actually paying a lot more than it was worth.

The turbary rights were worth something in times gone by, but not now. If you can't burn turf, she said, what was the use in having it?

*

In the half an hour before Barney was due, Cahir was writing lists. Making sure Dan would have everything. There wasn't much to pack and the two boys were quiet, making the odd joke about how it wasn't a wake. Why were they going on as if it was a wake?

Cahir was looking at his watch. Trying to judge when to give Dan his present or if it was so stupid that he shouldn't give it to him at all. At five to two, it was only fair to presume Barney would be on time.

Look, it's stupid, Cahir said. I made it from some plastic bottles. Remember that Lucozade bottle you had? I made a wee arm, see? You could put it in your room. I dunno.

Dan was smiling a big stupid smile. That's a good sign, Cahir thought. I don't even know if you like cats, he said, but they're good luck in China. The waving cats. Or, it might be Japan. Anyway, it's supposed to recharge in the sun, Cahir said, so that's something.

The tears couldn't be blinked back in, they rode a ball into Cahir's throat and couldn't be swallowed. Laughing burst out but the tears were tripping them until Barney's car swung into the front street, horn sounding. Three sharp sounds. Dan grabbed his bag. They embraced at the door and wished each other luck.

It's funny that Cahir always thought he was fine being alone but he couldn't know that. He wasn't alone until now.

Two shoots can grow from the same base and two crowns can sway happily in fine weather. But forked trees are inseparable. Inherently unstable. In a heavy wind, both crowns will sway too far. Back and forth. Apart. Creak, swaying in different directions until they crack. If you let it get as far as that, then both are doomed because the weaker side will fall immediately. It will snap and fall from the point where they diverge. The standing half will live longer but never fully recover. It will make some attempt to seal the wound. Exude sticky resinous pitch from the damaged site, try to keep water from collecting, from ingress and rot. It will be permanently weakened, much more easily hollowed from the inside out. It's better to disentangle before growing very high. It's better to get these things right early on. The development of proper structures is important for withstanding violent wind, heavy snow, great floods.

Cahir's face has healed up perfectly and his hand is nearly there. The new skin where the pulps were stitched together is a different texture than before. They say his fingerprints are different now. The tight concentric circles are interrupted, pulled asymmetric by blunt force and repair. A new set of identifying marks.

You never know what you can live with or live without. What'll turn out to be easy; wee buns; penny baps. Cahir is getting on fine. He can see himself clearly, getting on fine, bubbled up separate and looking reliable. Today, not a physical pain in his body, and it's an unplanned benefit of the digging, he thinks.

Eugene is moving on again and the glass is left shining. Purpose-driven, he keeps twisting his cloth, scouring filth from the windows and the sing-song, step-down bells ring over the Diamond.

The New Road

The lane is newly raked with stones. Coarse, blue, powdery stones, not very long dumped. The tread of heavy machinery hasn't weighed them in tight and Cahir can kick the top layer loose. The lane has been widened for diggers and vans. The hedgerow trees are cut and dug out. Wider, longer roads are how you settle new hills, how you surround and carve and dismantle a wild place. The untouched retreats, smaller and smaller, as roads creep and invade, as the last fence moves further out. All the scrub divisions and field boundaries are erased. The site is quiet on a Sunday morning, now the groundworks are over.

The blue chipped stones are better compacted at the new gate, splashing into the field like a driveway. There are no cars or vans and the excavator is silent. The machines have made tracks in the muck and lying water is cold but not frozen. There has been no frost yet. Glaucous tufts of grass drip with dew and sparkle under his gutties, cheap canvas not keeping damp from his socks. Cahir turns the bar of the gate and slides it back. The bolt clangs against the stop and he waits for what might be disturbed, watching for ramblers and surveyors before picking his way toward the new imprint.

The ground is dug up, poured with bind and aggregate, pillars driven into the earth to set and last a thousand years. White concrete setting in wooden collars and Cahir can stand inside their front door, raised up, for a look around. This is the sort of damage required if you want something to last. He can see the cows in the far field, the herd coming toward him slowly, hoping for food, unused to the new retaining wall.

The piles of dried wood are collected for removal. The soil is scraped clear. An attempt at neatness and order, to scour and dominate. A big skip is settled like a beached ship. Particles of foam insulation scatter like seeds over the ground. The blockwork of the walls is as high as the window frames and the big openings are supported by steel beams. All around the new building, rusted scaffolds clad the frame. Tom's house is built on the peak of the brow and from here he'll own what he can see. From here, he'll look out over a new canopy.

As the ground falls from Tom's house, on three sides falling from those foundations, there is growth. Hundreds and hundreds of newly planted saplings. Oak, ash, holly and birch, poking from mesh wire guards. The earth is moved and remade to hold them in the wilder areas below the house, where the gardens will drop into browning rushes and the rocky stream. He can't know which are his. Cahir has no way of picking them from the new planting. They are swallowed in new rows and grids, the new woods that will run the boundary of the stream and sweep over the rough slope, that will run in a narrow strip to the back gate of a small cottage. From the brow of the ridge, stood on the thick wooden planks of the scaffold, Cahir can see that the new wood starts at Lydia the Master's back door.

It's all changed and remade. They can't stop remaking it with diggers and trucks, spades and mixers. Cahir doesn't know where to look. It's hard for him to recognise the new shape of the place or to understand it as a place that has nothing to do with him. That it's Tom's house and Lydia's wood.

As the sun breaks through, apricity full on his face, the town is a series of shadows under him. He should go. Time moves faster on high ground. On a small slope hardly above the sea, time slipped Cahir by. At his work, he stopped listening to the noises below him but that didn't quieten them. In the near distance birds claim sharp calls, clean and bright and ordered out of the real world. If he listens, Cahir can hear the road and each step he takes out the lane, the noise of the road will get louder.

He tried his hardest to hold it in. He worked very hard to be good. Labouring and twisting and digging at the earth. Him and his knife letting blood to stream on the rocks. Wrecking. Control failing, the proof of it littered on the hillside. Fault and contrition inseparable, entangled, one unable to erase the other.

At the stream and its new planted bank, the water

splashes, gurgles and runs. The water that washes clean. The light is climbing at his back, rising over the town and the valley, streaming through the scaffolds.

The new growth is more than he could have done alone. He squats to take the dying leaves in hand, to pull the weeds and scrape the barks to check that sap is rising. He plants his hands on the damp soil and rubs his palms together until they are coated all over. The light shifts higher. Pouring cold, low, clear. High enough to light the woods.

Cahir's hands are among the new crowns. His eyes lift and dart over the hill. Intricate, gilt, it sweeps in front of him. It's all he can see.

The water runs and the birds call. The hill is not on fire. Unburnt hills are what are left of the world. The world is whatever can be saved.

Cahir says it over and over. He repeats and repeats what he wants to be true. On his lips and tongue, again and again until it feels like faith. Until he can almost believe that the road will stop here. That a small corner might stay whole.

He'll go now. It's not his. He has to pull his eyes away. Just a minute and then he'll go. One more look around him.

Over the water, the trees glint silver, almost white. They are hanging and dripping in red berries. Shiny crisp spheres fallen red on the soil, red and held up high. Picked at, caught, lit up.

Acknowledgements

Thanks: to Becky Walsh for reading in the first place, for giving me so much of her time and for leading me to the right places, for understanding what the story should be and for making it all real; to Lucy Luck for her insight on the text, her general advice, and for putting up with my clueless emails; to all at the *Stinging Fly* summer school but especially to Mia Gallagher because I'll be grateful forever; to my mum, dad, sisters and brothers, thank you for everything. We are lucky to share this life.

⒨RIGINALS

NEW WRITING FROM
BRITAIN'S OLDEST PUBLISHER

2020

Toto Among the Murderers | Sally J Morgan
An atmospheric debut novel set in 1970s Leeds and Sheffield
when attacks on women punctuated the news.

'An exhilarating novel'   Susan Barker

Self-Portrait in Black and White | Thomas Chatterton Williams
An interrogation of race and identity from one of America's
most brilliant cultural critics.

'An extraordinarily thought-provoking memoir'
                                                            Sunday Times

2019

Asghar and Zahra | Sameer Rahim
A tragicomic account of a doomed marriage.

'Funny and wise, and beautifully written'
                                    Colm Tóibín, *New Statesman*

Nobber | Oisín Fagan
A wildly inventive and audacious fourteenth-century Irish Plague novel.

'Vigorously, writhingly itself'   *Observer*, Books of the Year

2018
A Kind of Freedom | Margaret Wilkerson Sexton
A fascinating exploration of the long-lasting and enduring divisive legacy of slavery.

'A writer of uncommon nerve and talent'   *New York Times*

Jott | Sam Thompson
A story about friendship, madness and modernism.

'A complex, nuanced literary novel of extraordinary perception'   *Herald*

Game Theory | Thomas Jones
A comedy about friendship, sex and parenting, and about the games people play.

'Well observed and ruthlessly truthful'   *Daily Mail*

2017
Elmet | Fiona Mozley
An atmospheric Gothic fable about a family living on land that isn't theirs.

'A quiet explosion of a book, exquisite and unforgettable'
                                                    The Economist

2016

Blind Water Pass | Anna Metcalfe
A debut collection of stories about communication and miscommunication – between characters and across cultures.

'Demonstrates a grasp of storytelling beyond the expectations of any debut author'   *Observer*

The Bed Moved | Rebecca Schiff
Frank and irreverent, these stories offer a singular view of growing up (or not) and finding love (or not) in today's uncertain landscape.

'A fresh voice well worth listening to'   *Atlantic*

Marlow's Landing | Toby Vieira
A thrilling novel of diamonds, deceit and a trip up-river.

'Economical, accomplished and assured'   *The Times*

2015

An Account of the Decline of the Great Auk, According to One Who Saw It | Jessie Greengrass

The twelve stories in this startling collection range over centuries and across the world.

'Spectacularly accomplished'   *The Economist*

Generation | Paula McGrath
An ambitious novel spanning generations and continents on an epic scale.

'A hugely impressive and compelling narrative'
John Boyne, *Irish Times*